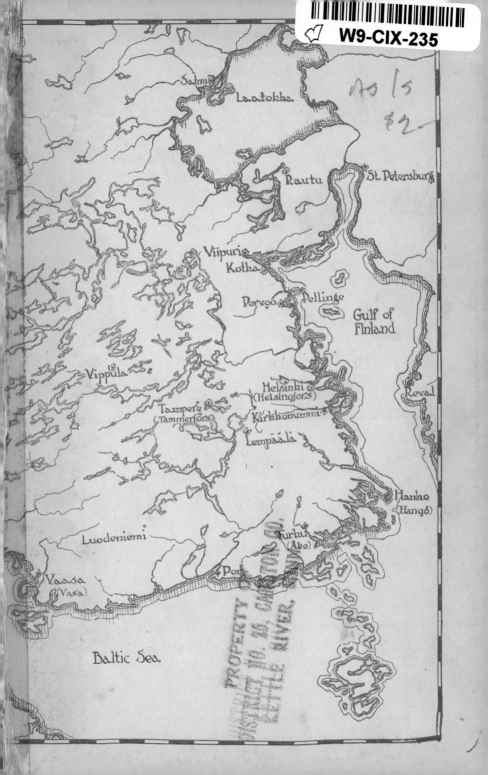

Salmi

La.a.tokha.

Rautu

St. Petersburg

Viipuri

Kotka.

Porvoo

Pellinge

Gulf of Finland

Vippula

Helsinki
(Helsingfors)

Reval

Tampere
(Tammerfors)

Kirkkonummi

Lempäälä

Hanko
(Hangö)

Luodeniemi

Turku
(Åbo)

Vaasa
(Vasa)

Pori

Baltic Sea.

VAINO
A Boy of New Finland

JULIA DAVIS ADAMS *has also written*

THE SWORDS OF THE VIKINGS

"Here is a book so quietly beautiful in all the features that mark good book-making that we wish it might fall to the lot of every child who reads to have it to mull over and fondle page by page until it becomes his touchstone of what a book should be.

"It is surprising what variety of circumstance and situation and character appear in these old tales whose themes are so many of them similar. The total impression is one of vigor, humor, and beauty. And the beauty of the translation should be stressed; for its simplicity is a matter of genuine distinction, not a pose assumed for children."— Anna Speed Brackett in *The Saturday Review of Literature.*

"*The Swords of the Vikings,* by Julia Davis Adams, will no doubt go into all our public libraries, for it is a volume of versions of sections from the writings of the ancient Danish chronicler Saxo Grammaticus, a writer whose importance is far greater than many of us may realize today. . . . These short tales make fine reading aloud. . . ."— May Lamberton Becker in *The American Girl.*

"Such tales, out of a simpler world than ours and concerned with human nature stripped to its essentials, offer a welcome relief from the fiction of the day."—John G. Neihardt in the *St. Louis Post-Dispatch.*

"In the days of the Vikings there was no dearth of reckless adventure. Indeed there was more of that than of anything else. *The Swords of the Vikings* gives one a good idea of life in those stirring times."—*John Martin's Book.*

Published by E. P. DUTTON & CO., INC.

On the Glorious Sixteenth of May, Mannerheim Entered Helsingfors
at the Head of His Victorious Army

VAINO

A Boy of New Finland

by

JULIA DAVIS ADAMS

Author of "The Swords of the Vikings"

Illustrated by Lempi Ostman

E. P. DUTTON & CO., INC.
NEW YORK

20

FIRST PRINTING ....AUGUST, 1929
SECOND PRINTING ....AUGUST, 1929
THIRD PRINTING ....NOVEMBER, 1931

TO
BILLY

Contents

Contents

List of Illustrations

[ix]

Illustrations

Author's Foreword

EVERYONE has heard of Nurmi, the "flying Finn," the Olympic runner, but not everyone has more than a vague impression of his country, an impression of isolation, and forbidding cold. In the course of a series of visits to Finland between 1923 and 1926, I learned to have a deep appreciation of the somberly heroic spirit of her people, the spirit that has enabled them to change themselves in five short years from a nation which had been subject for centuries to a succession of foreign powers, into a soundly established and quietly thriving Republic. In every field Finland has made amazing strides during her brief independence, in architecture, art, social legislation, athletics. Ten years ago organized sports were not allowed in Finland.

Her recent Olympic Game record needs no comment.

The Finnish people differ from other Scandinavians in being of Magyar extraction, related in race and tongue to the Hungarians, but they have now a strong admixture of Swedish blood, a heritage of the centuries when they were ruled by Sweden, and they are bilingual.

In adapting their legends, so deeply expressive of the vein of poetry, of wildness, of magical sadness, which is in every Finnish soul, it seemed unfortunate to omit their stirring modern history, and consequently I have endeavored to weave the two together. The modern part of the work is as historically accurate as possible, and a number of the war incidents are based on experiences of Finnish friends.

Such a blending is typical of the Finnish character, in which, side by side with obstinate endurance, a smouldering passion of patriotism never absent from their thoughts,

an indefatigable quiet acceptance of hard-
ships, there exists so much love of beauty,
and poetical imagination, flaring out in
their folk songs and stories.

The legends are complete in themselves,
as is the account of the Red Revolution.
Either may be read separately, but both are
necessary for a true understanding of the
Finnish people.

VAINO

A Boy of New Finland

I

Under Hooves

IT was four o'clock of an October afternoon in 1916. A few snowflakes fell through the woods out of a leaden sky. Winter was stalking down on Finland from the North.

Vaino Lundborg trotted along the pine covered road, swinging his schoolbooks at the end of a strap. Twice every day he travelled this kilo. Every morning he took the blue tram to Helsingfors, where he went to school. Every evening he got off at the last stop, and followed the narrow road to his home. Usually he had company, his sister Anniki, who was eighteen and a student at the University, or his brother Sven, who was twenty and knew almost everything, but today he was alone. In autumn or late spring he ran all the way as part of the training he had laid out for himself, and when the soft thick snow came to stay he went over it on skis. Some of the boys at school thought that it must be hard to have so far to go, but Vaino was like his country-bred mother, and would not stay in the city longer than necessary.

Vaino loved the road. He knew every meter of it as he knew his own home. He knew where the squirrels nested in the fallen hemlock, and where the round-eyed rabbits crouched hiding in the thickets. Even in winter, when the afternoons were dark, he never felt afraid there. It was all as safe and familiar as his own bed.

He sang as he went, one of the sadly gay

old Finnish songs, a song he had learned from his mother. It made him think of her, and of the bright fire that would be burning in the tiled stove when he reached home. Vaino liked to sing.

A sudden beating of furious hooves sounded down the road. A Russian officer on a high black horse dashed around the corner, the skirts of his overcoat flying out behind him. Vaino had to jump into a tangle of brambles to save himself from being ridden down. He dropped his books in his excitement, and when he stooped to pick them up the briars scratched his hand.

The Russian officer reined the black horse onto its haunches so that its forelegs pawed the air, and whirling in the path came back to Vaino.

"So it was you, making that horrible noise?" he asked in Russian. Vaino understood that language, but he raised an expressionless face. The black horse pranced to and fro, the officer held him in, and went on,

jokingly, "Singing dismal songs in a barba-
rous language!"

Vaino looked more stupid than ever if possible, and the officer dropped into Swedish,
which he spoke with a bad accent.

"It is amazing that you do not know Russian. You had better learn it. Come to me at
the barracks in town, and I will teach you
something really gay. Your voice isn't bad,
but it needs training."

Vaino stared up at him sullenly. The officer was a handsome young man, with wild
black eyes, and a little silky moustache, and
he was very smart. Everything about him,
from buckles to boots, glittered and shone.
Vaino hated him.

"Tch!" said the Russian, "I can see that
you are just another thick-headed Finn. Next
time, get out of the way more quickly when
you see me coming. I nearly ran over you."

He cracked his whip in the air until it
whistled over Vaino's head, and the black
horse bounded away. Vaino caught up his

books, and ran home so fast that his lungs were nearly bursting when he came there.

His mother listened quietly while he told her what had happened. When he finished she put her arm around him, and drew him to her, saying only, "I am glad Anniki was not with you," while her eyes burned with that somber flame which he had often seen there.

That evening, as on many evenings, the family sat about the stove. Anniki, drawing her heavy brows together, stared into the fire. Sven, at the center table, was working with compass and square. Their mother knitted, and as her fingers moved, she told them one of the legends of Finland. The older children knew them, by heart.

It was for Vaino that she told them now, with his head resting against her knee, Vaino, who showed the Swedish descent of his father in his blue eyes and ruddy skin, and bore the most deeply Finnish name which his mother could give him.

The mother's soft voice rippled through the room, speaking in melodious Finnish, telling one of the tales which are songs, the songs which are stories.

The Beginning

These are the songs which were taught to the people of Suomi, the Marshland, the land of the Finns; taught by the wind which whispered through the needles of the pines, taught by the water as it lapped their thousand shores, by the frost, when the bays groaned in its hold, by the birds singing in the brief sweet summer.

The fathers of the people sang these songs, carving their axe hafts, and knife handles through the long winter evenings, and the mothers of the people crooned them at their spinning wheels.

The first song tells of the beginning.

Long, long ago, before there was anything, Ilmatar, daughter of the air, wearied at her loneliness in the vast and empty spaces from the sky to the edge of the sky. Like a shooting star, like a comet with a fiery tail, she plunged from the high blue sky into the deep blue sea, and there the caressing of the waves brought a child to life within her.

For seven times one hundred years, Ilmatar swam to and fro, finding no land where her weary body might rest, nor any living thing to bear her company. At last in her loneliness and her pain, she called to Ukko, god of the Thunder.

"Highest of gods, whom I rashly left, when I ceased to tread the air under my feet, come where thou art needed!"

No answer came from the high blue sky, but soon a pearly seagull floated down, and darted over the waves seeking a place to rest. Ilmatar raised her knee above the water. Upon this smooth and round white hill the seagull built a warm round nest, and laid in it six eggs of gold, and a seventh egg of iron.

For six days it sat upon them, until on the seventh the warmth of its body burnt through the nest, Ilmatar flinched, the eggs fell from her knee, and broke into a thousand pieces.

From the lower shell was formed the earth, and from the upper shell the heavens which arch above the earth. The yolk of a golden egg made the blazing sun, and the white of a golden egg the silver gleaming moon. From the mottled parts came the bright little stars, and from the darkish parts the high sailing clouds.

In this way the world was made.

Again for years, Ilmatar, the water mother, floated hither and yon, moulding the earth. With her mighty hands she wrought out bays and headlands, high mountains of twisted rock, caves for fishes, deep down where her white feet rested, and coves for netting salmon.

The long years passed.

Within Ilmatar her child Vainomoinen,

the aged and the ageless, the mighty singer, wearied of his dark resting place.

"Sun of the day," he cried, "and moon of the night, and Great Bear, the dog of heaven, hear me, and free me, that I may look upon your splendour."

There came no answer from the Sun, nor the Moon, nor the Great Bear.

Then Vaino took the fourth finger of his left hand, the nameless finger, opened the portal of his resting place, and swam out into the sea.

Nine years he swam, his long white beard mingling with the white crested billows, until he came to a bare and rocky headland. He pulled himself out of the water, and resting on his knees looked into the heavens. Then he was warmed by the silver sun, and cooled by the golden moon, and beheld for the first time the Great Bear, circling about the North Star, the nail of heaven, which holds up the dark blue canopy of the midnight sky.

Vaino sat in thought on the silent headland, and all around him was waste. There
were no whispering trees, no waving grass,
nor any voice of bird to break his thought.
At last he rose, and called on Sampsa, the
child of earth, and Sampsa came to sow the
land, swinging his arms as he scattered the
seeds far and wide in the empty spaces.

He sowed pine on the hills, fir on the
knolls, heather in the sand, and slender birch
and alder in the dales. He sowed cherries
where the ground was sour, willows in the
marshes, juniper amid the rocks, and oaks
beside the rivers.

All the sowing grew and flourished, while
Vaino watched it, save the oak, the tree of the
highest and greatest god. Then five maidens
rose from the water, moved the grass and
burnt it, set the acorn in the ashes, and the
oak took root and grew.

Higher and higher it grew, put forth one
hundred branches, and shut out the light of
the sun and the moon, so that men on the

earth, and fishes in the water, went in darkness and could not tell day from night. On all the earth no man was strong enough to fell it.

"Mother Ilmatar," cried Vaino, standing on the shore, and stretching out his arms over the sea, "send a power from the floor of the ocean to hew down this oak, and restore to us the light of the sun and the moon."

So for a long, long time he stood, with the sea wind tossing his long white beard in the unchanging twilight, until at last there was Something, skipping along over the surface of the waves. Nearer and nearer it came, and Vaino saw that it was a tiny man, no longer than a thumb. On his head was a bright red copper helmet, on his feet were bright red copper boots, and he wore a belt of copper, turned green by the sea. He skipped out of the water, climbed the pebbles, and stood before Vaino.

"What are you, little creature?" asked Vaino, looking down.

"I am the hero of Ocean, who will fell the oak," piped the tiny man.

Vaino looked up, up, up, into the green canopy above him, and as far as his eyes could reach, he saw nothing but waving leaves. Then he looked down at the red copper helmet, bobbing about his ankles, and said, gravely,

"You are not equal to it."

No sooner had he uttered these words, than the little man began to grow. Soon he met Vaino eye to eye, soon his head was lost in the clouds, while his feet were stamping the ground, and the width of his mouth was a fathom. On seven stones he whetted his copper axe, in three strides he reached the center of the land. Three blows he struck at the oak, and at the third, flame burst from his axe. With a splitting, and a groaning, and a crashing, the great tree tottered to the ground, and the ground trembled at its fall.

The sun shone, the moon glimmered as before, and the people gathered around the

SOON HIS HEAD WAS LOST IN THE CLOUDS

oak tree, chattering and filled with wonder.
Those who tore off a branch were blessed
with riches, those who took a leaf from the
very top became magic-working shamen, but
those who were content with a simple twig
were lucky in love.

Now the birds sang in the trees, and the
flowers blossomed in the meadows, and the
berries bore fruit in the thickets, but the people were hungry, for there was no grain from
which to make them bread.

Day after day, Vaino wandered, lost in
thought, by the blue edge of the sea, around
and around the land, and back again. One
morning he found seven grains of barley on
the sand. He took them up, and put them
in his squirrel-leg pouch. As he went with
them into the woods, stooping to look at the
ground and find a place for sowing, he heard
the titmouse chirp from a nearby tree:

"Barley will not grow, while the forest
stands.

The ground must be burnt, and tilled by human hands."

Then Vaino sharpened his axe, and laid about him to left and right, with his white beard streaming out behind him as he strode along, felling the trees of the forest one after another. But he spared the slender birch for the birds to rest in.

Now the forest was felled, but Vaino leaned on his axe, thinking, for he had no fire with which to burn the ground. An eagle soared down from the clouds, and said, "Why did you spare the birch, Vaino, and stop with your task unfinished?"

"I left the birch for the birds of the air, and the kingly eagle to rest in," said Vaino.

The eagle was so pleased with this answer, that he soared back out of sight in the clouds, and catching the crooked snake of lightning in his beak, brought it down to the earth. When the fire had swept over the fallen trees and burnt them to ashes, the blackened ground was smooth for the sowing.

Vaino reached into his squirrel-skin pouch, took out the seven seeds and planted them. Each time he stooped to put one in the ground he prayed:

"Ancient Earth Mother, stir in thy slumber, and return me this grain a hundred-fold."

After he had covered each seed, he stood up, and raising his arms to the sky, cried:

"Ukko, god of clouds and thunder, send rain, grow grain."

A cloud floated through the sky, from the north, one from the south, from the east and from the west. They joined their edges so that no light shone between them, and the rain fell, soft and sweet as honey.

Seven days later, Vaino went to the field, and all the place where the forest had been was covered with tender shoots of growing grain. Behind him called the soft voiced cuckoo, harbinger of spring.

"Why did you leave the birch tree standing, O Vaino?" fluted the cuckoo.

"For thy pleasure, Cuckoo, so that the silver notes from thy sand-colored throat might ring at morning and at evening and at noon over the meadows, bringing joy to our hearts, and plenty to our harvests."

Then the cuckoo sang in gratitude, and there was no sorrow anywhere, for Vaino, the old and faithful, had brought light, and spring, and food, to his people.

———

The mother's voice trailed into silence. Anniki stretched her arms up to her head, where the dark brown braids were bound in a smooth coronet, and spoke:

"Scarelius says that it is mothers like you, who keep the music alive in the hearts of the Finnish people."

Sven looked up, half laughing, from his work.

"Scarelius is the wisest young man in the University, of course. Has he finished his concerto, and what is he going to do?"

"He is going to Germany next month." answered Anniki, darkly, and there was a catch in her voice. "He thinks the time is very near."

The mother rose. "Don't tease your sister, Sven. Vaino, it is time for small children to go to bed."

"I am not a small child, Mother. I can outrun any of the boys in the class above me."

"Don't let the Russians catch you at it," said Sven bitterly. "They don't encourage the Finns to have sports, you know."

Fru Lundborg sighed. Her face was in shadow, but the soft glow of the lamp shone on her figure, deep bosomed, square shouldered, firmly planted, and on her strong quiet hands. She was a patient woman of fixed purpose.

She took a candle, lit it, and handed it to Vaino. He took it and left the room without further protest, but after he had climbed into his bed, that was built into the wall in imitation of the peasant beds, he lay awake for a long time, thinking.

There was a great deal to think about. Why should the Russians mind if a boy practised running? Why had the teachers at school been forbidden to speak Finnish? Why had his own mother's brother, Uncle Paavo, from near Tammerfors, been sent to a place called Siberia for making speeches?

Vaino heard a great deal about the Russians. Sven and Anniki were always bringing home friends from the University who would sit late by the fire, talking in excited undertones. One phrase ran through their speech like the refrain of a song,—"if we were free—when we are free." Mother sighed as she listened to them, and sometimes she said, "It won't be so easy, young hotheads," but she never tried to stop them, and that deep flame burnt in her eyes while they talked. Vaino understood that he must never repeat anything which they said.

It seemed that there was always someone

for the Finns to hate. In the old legends it had been the Lapps, and then it had been the Swedes, but nobody had minded about that for centuries, and the Swedes in the country had become the most patriotic Finns. Now, ever since anybody could remember, it was the Russians.

Finally Vaino fell asleep, to dream of a procession of Russian officers, riding black against a windy sky, while the hard hooves of their horses trampled Finnish earth.

The Russian Officer

IT WAS in the following March that Sven appeared one morning at Vaino's school, and said that he had come to take him home. Vaino did not like to ask questions in front of the other boys, so he collected his books, his fur cap and gloves and his coat without saying anything. Sven led the way out to a drosky sleigh, with a row of bells jingling on the high yoke over the horse.

"Are we really going home in that?" asked Vaino in astonishment.

"You are," answered Sven, smiling in an excited way. "I must stay in town. Here is a letter for Mother. This driver is a friend of mine, and will take good care of you."

"But what has happened?" asked Vaino. Sven came closer, pretending to tuck the rug around his knees, and spoke in a low voice which sounded very earnest although his eyes were shining.

"There has been a revolution in Russia, led by a man called Kerensky. The Tsar has been put out."

If anybody but Sven had said so, Vaino could not have believed it, for it sounded impossible. Even so it seemed very remote, and he could not see what it had to do with him.

"Why should I have to go home?"

"Nobody knows what may happen," answered Sven. "The Russian soldiers and sailors here are excited. Their officers were the Tsar's men, and now they have no more authority. There may be riots. I am needed in town. Anniki has gone to Scarelius's

people, since he is in Germany, and you must
go home and look after Mother."

That settled it, although Vaino thought
that he would have liked to see a riot. He had
one more question.

"Will it be good for Finland?"

Sven threw back his head, his broad face
beaming. "We think it is the beginning of
everything!"

"Hurrah!" shouted Vaino. As the sleigh
started off he stood up in it waving his arms
at Sven, who watched him out of sight and
waved back to him. "Hurrah! Hurrah!"

Vaino drew the fur rugs up to his nose,
and enjoyed watching the shiny snow all the
way home. Still more he enjoyed bursting in
on his mother as she sat sewing by the stove,
and shouting the news. She called the driver
in for a cup of coffee before he started back,
and she gave Vaino a glass of milk and some
black bread with cheese. When she had read
Sven's letter carefully she began asking the
driver a great many questions.

The driver liked drinking coffee by a fire and giving information. He told how the soldiers and sailors were getting together in little knots all over town, with all the raggle-taggle of Helsingfors, and some of the Finnish workmen, more shame to them, who had been helping the Russians build the fortifications.

"A fine lot of friends they've made," he said, "There is too much shouting, and too much aquavit." He threw up his hand as if he were emptying a glass down his throat.

"What do they say?" asked Fru Lundborg.

"The usual stuff. 'Down with the rich—down with the officers.' They are starting to look for the officers."

"What do they mean to do?"

The driver said nothing, but he drew the edge of his hand across his throat. After a silence he got up, wiped his long moustache, and saying many times, "Thanks for the

[25]

food, gracious lady," bowed himself backwards out of the door.

Fru Lundborg and Vaino returned to the fire in the living room. She did not sit down as usual, but paced to and fro. She made Vaino tell her again just what Sven had said, how he had looked. She re-read his letter, and dropped it into the fire. At last she drew up a chair, and folded her hands in her lap. Vaino saw that her knuckles were white. He did not know what to do with himself, and she took no notice of him. He went to the window and looked out, started whistling and came back to the fire. Finally he said that he thought he would run out for a couple of hours' skiing before it grew dark.

"Son," answered his mother, "Sven sent you out to take care of me, didn't he?"

"Yes."

"Then I should rather not have you go out alone this afternoon, and I should rather not stay alone."

Vaino sat down again, and she smiled at him tenderly.

"I'll make it as easy as I can for you. Get the pinewood you were carving, and I will tell you a story while I sew."

When they were both comfortably settled, the mother began.

The War of Song

Vaino, the old and faithful, dwelt in the meadows which his hands had sown, singing by day and by night the songs which his wisdom had taught him. Mighty songs, they were, wonder-working songs, songs which a dying race has forgotten.

The news of his singing sped to Pohjola, the northland, where the somber Lapps dwell in changeless day or changeless night. The old men of the village sat and shook their heads about the fire, and cackled at a youth with a frown on his flat yellow face.

"You call yourself a singer, Joukahainen,"

they snickered, "but there is a man in Suomi who can sing the barley into the fields, and the berries onto the bushes."

Jouka sprang up in a rage, flung himself out of the wigwam-like house, and rushed home to his mother.

"Say farewell to me, Mother," he shouted, "for I am off to Suomi to show this old man how to sing!"

"Son, Son," cried his father and his mother together, "Don't try to sing against Vaino, for he will send you to a bed beneath the snow."

"My father is wise, and my mother is wiser, but I am the wisest of all, so just watch me sing old Vaino into a coffin of stone."

With that Jouka ran to his white spotted horse, with the fiery eyes, and the spark-casting hooves, and hitched it to his gold-bedecked sleigh. He cracked his red-beaded whip in the frosty air, and set off, shouting, for Suomi.

For three days he thundered along, with

the runners of his sledge rattling over the sweet brown earth, where it showed between the patches of snow. On the fourth day, he came with a flourish to the meadows of Suomi, where the road ran beside the lake, with the tall pines shedding needles over it, and the fields beyond.

Along the narrow road, Vaino himself was driving peacefully, in a broad low sleigh, with a little cream-colored pony, and a new song of magic growing in his heart.

Crack! went Jouka's whip, his horse plunged forward, and crashed his sledge into the sledge of Vaino. The shafts and the runners rammed fast together, the splinters flew, and the steam from the quivering horses made a light mist in the blue air.

Vaino roused from his revery, and said mildly, "Thoughtless boy, why do you not look where you are going? Just see, the runners and shafts of my sleigh, my fine sleigh, are broken."

Jouka tossed his black hair in the wind, and laughed with his wide red mouth, shouting, "I am Jouka, the famous singer! What sort of a place do you come from, old man?"

"I am Vaino," answered the other, patiently, "and now be good enough to make way for your elders, my boy."

"Age makes no difference here," cried Jouka, "only wisdom matters. If you are really Vaino, I will sing against you, and we shall see who will win the singing."

"I am an old man, who lives in the meadows, and knows only the song of the cuckoo, as it calls from the edge of the woods," said Vaino, quietly, "so let us first hear how much you know."

Jouka planted his feet wide apart in his sledge, and began.

"Oh, I know so much, so very much,
    which my cleverness shows to me!
I know that smoke goes out through a
    hole in the roof, and that salmon
    swim in the sea,

And that up in the North, where the
    ground is hard, the reindeer draw the
    plow,
And the mare in the South, and the elk
    for the Lapps.
What more would you like to hear
    now?"

"Well," said Vaino, "I have heard children prattle like that, but not grown men.
Sing to me now of eternal things."

Jouka cracked his red and blue whip, and
began again.

"The titmouse is a bird, and the viper is
    a snake.
Iron is hard, and the fire will burn and
    bake.
Water will cure, as it springs from a
    stone.
The willow was the first tree, and not
    that alone,
But pineroots made the first house, and
    the first pot was stone."

"Well," sighed Vaino, looking off over
the smiling meadows as they threw off their

winter coat, "is that all, or are you going to
tell me some more nonsense?"

Jouka laid down his whip, planted himself
more firmly in the sledge, and sang until his
voice cracked.

"There are other little things, which I
    remember now,
  For I am the man who made the ocean
    with a plow.
  I piled up the hills, and I dug out the
    caves,
  Where the fishes live, underneath the
    waves.
  I planted crystal pillars to hold up the
    sky,
  And scattered the stars, where you see
    them on high."

"What lies you tell," said Vaino, mildly.
"Nobody had ever seen you, nobody had ever
heard of you, nobody had ever thought of
you, when the hills were piled up, and the
sky was arched on its crystal pillars."

"Very well," screamed Jouka. "If you do
not like my singing, try my sword!"

"I cannot fight with a child," replied Vaino, softly.

Then Jouka twisted his mouth to one side of his flat yellow face and yelped, furiously, "Look out, old man, for I sing people who are afraid to fight with me into swine, and chase them squealing around the cowyard!"

Now a slow wrath stirred in Vaino, and he lifted his face to the sky, and began to sing. Clear and soft were the songs he sang, but the earth trembled beneath him, the copper-filled mountains trembled about him, and the very stones on the shore split in pieces. Vaino sang, but today the dying race has lost even the echoes of his songs.

Very slowly and softly, Vaino began to sing of Jouka.

The runners sprang from Jouka's sledge and grew up as saplings on either side of the road, the gilded sleigh tumbled into the lake, the beribboned whip turned into a reed on the water's edge, and the white-spotted horse became a stone.

Jouka stood alone in the middle of the road, and wished that he dared run away.

Vaino stretched out his hands toward Jouka, and went on singing, never louder, never faster.

Jouka's sword left his hands, to flash like lightning in the heavens, his crossbow bent like a rainbow over the lake, his flying arrows soared up and turned into hawks that whirled about him. While he trembled, his cap floated from his head, and became a cloud in the sky, his gloves sailed off his hands, to be waterlilies on the surface of the lake.

Then Jouka would have run away, but his feet were like stones and he could not lift them.

Vaino's song went on, and now it came from all directions at once, and Jouka found himself sinking slowly in the black spring mud by the water's edge. Now indeed he opened his wide red mouth, and shrieked at the top of his lungs."

"O, wise Vaino, good Vaino, sing your

songs backwards! Sing your songs backwards, and I will give you something rich and rare!"

"What will it be?" asked Vaino, but he wove the words into his song so that he never stopped singing.

"Take one of my beautiful crossbows," said Jouka, sinking up to his knees, "for one is swift, and the other is sure, and you may have whichever you like."

"My house is filled with bows which hunt by themselves in the woods so that I need not even bend them," answered Vaino, and he went on singing.

"Take one of my boats," cried Jouka, with the mud up to his waist, "for one can race, and the other can carry anything, and you may have whichever you like."

"I have plenty of boats," answered Vaino, "some that sail with the wind, and some that sail against it," and he went on singing.

"Take one of my horses," shouted Jouka, waving his arms, with the mud up to his armpits, "for one can pull, and the other can run, and you may have whichever you like."

"My stalls are full of white-footed horses," answered Vaino, "so nice and fat that their backs will hold water," and he went on singing.

"Vaino, Vaino," sobbed Jouka, "sing your songs backwards, and I will give you a golden helmet, and a hat full of silver which my father won in battle."

"All my chests," said Vaino, smiling, "are filled with gold as old as the moon, and with silver as old as the sun," and he went on singing.

"Vaino," pled Jouka, with the mud up to his chin, "take my fields and houses and everything that I have, only spare my life."

"My own fields are better," answered Vaino, "and I have plenty of them."

Now the mud was up to Jouka's mouth, and he rolled his little black eyes to and fro, and cried in despair.

"Vaino, Vaino, take my little sister, my

lovely little sister, Aino. She will dust for you, and wash for you, and sweep, and bake and weave, and look after the milk."

Then Vaino stopped his singing, and sat down with a smile on a stone by the side of the road to rest himself. After a minute he began peacefully with the very note on which he had left off, to sing his song backwards.

First Jouka rose from the mud, and saw his weapons and clothes floating back to him from the sky. Then the sleigh stood on the road again, and the horse snorted beside it. Sadly he got in the sleigh, and sadly and silently he drove away from old Vaino, who sat smiling by the lake.

When he came within sight of home, after his long drive, he whipped up his horse, and dashed against the doorway with such force that he broke his sledge in pieces. Out ran his father and his mother.

"Son, Son," they cried, "whatever did you do that for?"

Jouka turned his face away from them, and rubbed his fur sleeves over his tearful eyes.

"Now dear little son," said his mother, "what is the matter?"

"O, Mother, Mother," answered Jouka, "there is nothing but sorrow for me all the rest of my life, for the magician Vaino overcame me, and I have had to promise him Aino, our little Aino, to tend him in his old age!"

"Why, Jouka," cried his mother, rising joyfully on the tips of her toes, "why in the world do you cry over that? I could wish nothing better for our little Aino! It is the grandest marriage she could make, and none would bring us greater honor!"

But when Aino heard him, she crept away silently, and her mother found her sobbing in a heap by the threshold.

"Now, Aino," she said tenderly, "you must not be a silly little girl, for you will have a noble husband, and a fine house, with perhaps a window in it, so that you can sit on a bench and look out."

"Mother," sobbed Aino, "I am too young to put up my long hair, and be a wife in a strange country, away from the sun and the moon, and my brother's little workroom, where I have been so happy."

Then her mother laughed, and pulled her to her feet, saying, "Most foolish little daughter, do you not know that berries grow on bushes even outside your father's pastures, and that the sun and the moon shine on every land?"

Aino smiled at her mother through her tears, and tried to look gay, but when no one was watching her, she ran off into the woods, to be alone with her grief.

II

She hurried along the shaded path to the woods, blinking the tears from her eyes. When she heard the birds calling among the dimly-lit pines, and trod the fragrant

needles, she felt that no harm could come to
her there, and fell to stripping sharp little
twigs from the white birches for bath
whisks.

> "Here is one for my father, and one for
>   my mother,
>   And with this I'll make ruddy the skin
>   of my brother."

She sang to herself, picturing the steam rising from the hot stones in the bath-house, and
feeling the refreshing sting of the whisk
against her round little legs.

Singing she turned homeward through the
elder thickets, and suddenly stood face to
face with old Vaino, who had come to Lapland in search of her.

He looked with delight at the slim young
maiden, with the flowing hair and the
startled eyes, and he caught her round brown
wrist in one wrinkled hand, while with the
other he fumbled in his squirrelskin pouch.
Out came a silver chain, with a silver cross,
which he hung around her neck, and a bright

red ribbon which he wound in her hair. He brushed his long white beard out of his mouth, and said, gently,

"Lovely little Aino, wear for me, and for no other, the silver cross on your breast, and the ribbon wound in your hair."

But Aino wrenched herself away from him, and answered with quivering lips, "I will not wear them for you, nor for anyone else, for I love the dresses my mother weaves for me better than fine robes from over the water, and I would rather eat black crusts with my father than white bread in the house of a stranger."

Then she tore the silver necklace from her neck, and the red ribbon from her hair, and flinging them into the bushes, ran home through the woods, sobbing aloud as she ran.

On the log that was the threshold sat her father, carving a handle for his hatchet, and he looked at her tear-stained face.

"Why do you weep my daughter?" he called, "you are too young for sorrow."

"Reason enough, dear father," she sobbed as she ran past him, "for I have lost my silver beads, and a red ribbon from my hair."

At the gate sat Jouka, fashioning new runners for his sledge in place of the ones he had broken. He heard the thudding of her bare feet, and asked,

"Why do you weep, poor sister? You are too young for sorrow."

"Reason enough, dear brother," she cried without stopping, "for I have lost my silver beads, and the red ribbon from my hair."

She sped on, like a flying wild thing, seeking the only shelter it knows, to the milk house, where her mother was skimming the golden cream.

"Why do you weep, little daughter?" said her mother, "you are too young for sorrow."

Aino ran into her arms, sobbing wildly.

"Mother, mother, I have just met Vaino in the wood, and he hung a silver cross about my neck, and wound a red ribbon in my hair, and bade me wear them for him and for no other. But I tore them off, and threw them away, and I told him that I loved my homespun better than all that he could bring me, and that I could never never leave my father, and my dear dear mother!"

Her mother sat down on a bench by the milk house, and took both her hands, saying,

"Dry your young eyes, my pretty darling. All this year you shall eat fresh butter, and pork next year, and cream cakes the year after, until you are the plumpest prettiest bride in the world. And now if you will listen, I will tell you where to find your bridal dress.

"Up on the mountain, where the trees are bent before the North Wind, there is a log store-house. In the store-house there is a room, and in the room there is a chest, hollowed out of a single tree, and painted in the brightest colors. When you raise the heavy creaking lid, you will find inside six golden girdles, and seven sky-blue robes, and I will tell you how they came there.

"Long, long ago, when I was a maid, and ran berrying in the thickets, I came to a place at the edge of the woods, where the pines bathed their branches in the water, and the ferns grew thick, and there I saw the daughter of the moon, weaving a girdle, and the daughter of the sun, spinning thread for a robe.

"I tiptoed over the little flowers that grew amid the pine needles, and when I came up to them, I clasped my hands, and said, 'Moonlight's daughter, give your gold, and Sunlight's daughter, give your silver, to this poor little maid who has no dower.'

"Then, while I knelt on the moss before them, the gold of the moonlight decked my throat and my waist, and the silver of the sun touched my head, and they wove me a robe, blue like the sky, and a shift of linen, white as sun-kissed snow.

"When I danced home to my father I was like a summer flower. For three days everyone exclaimed over me, but on the third I took my fine garments up the high mountain, and laid them in the painted chest in the room of the storehouse, for I meant that no one should have them save my own dear little daughter who would come to me some day.

"Now you must go to the chest, and tie the silk ribbons about your forehead, and hang the golden cross of the moon on your breast, and don the shift of linen, and the woolen kirtle, and the silken belt. Then you will be the most beautiful bride in the world, like a little red raspberry growing on the mountain, and all your family will be filled with pride."

As she spoke, her mother led little Aino through the yard, patting her cheeks, and set her on the mountain path. Then she went back to skimming the golden cream, smiling to think that the maid should not know what was good for her.

Little Aino climbed the path slowly, up beyond the last tree which the North Wind had twisted, and her tears fell on the lichen-covered stones, for she no longer troubled to wipe them away. As she went she said to herself.

"In the days which I have forgotten, my heart danced like a wave, but now it is frozen in the black grave of sorrow.

"If I had died in being born, a few feet of earth would have been enough for me, and a few tears would my mother have shed, and Jouka, none at all.

"Now, rather than serve an old man, an old man whom I do not know, I should like to lie under the rippling lake, with the fishes my only companions."

By this time she had come to the store-house, and into the dusty room. When she saw the beautiful things inside the painted chest, for a moment she forgot to weep. She put on the finest of seven fine blue robes, and tied it around her waist with a girdle of gold. She bound silver disks on her forehead with ribbons of scarlet and blue, and put on the white woolen stockings, and a pair of little fur shoes. She spread out her arms, and turned herself about, thinking, "If only I could see myself! I will run and look in the glassy lake."

But when she came out of the house, and remembered why she had been given these fine things, her head felt as if she were carrying a stone on it, her feet grew too heavy to dance down the path, and she said to herself,

"If in a little while my way should lead
 To dark Tuonela, the land of the dead,
  Who would shed tears for me?

"Neither my father, nor brother, nor
  mother.
 I could lie quietly in the black mud,
  With the fishes above me."

So she wandered through the wood, not caring where her feet might lead her, not noticing the short hour of night, nor that the dawn had come again. At last she found herself on the border of a wide lake, reed-fringed. Far away she saw, or thought she saw, three maidens bathing in the water, and then she thought that they must be only three slim white birches on the far dim shore.

She took off her robe, blue as the sky, and laid it on a willow, and she let her snowy shift, her stockings and shoes, and the ribbons that bound her hair, all drop on the pebbles. Like a plump little seal she slid into the cold spring water, and swam toward a rock in the distant center. There were tiny bits of thin ice floating about, and as she swam she felt the weight of her heart pulling her under the waves, and her arms growing more and more weary.

"I came here to bathe," she said, "but now I am lost, like a dove fallen out of the nest. Never more may my father cast his net in these wide blue waters, nor my mother moisten her baking, nor my brother bring his pony here to drink. For the water of the lake will be the blood from my veins, and the fish my flesh, and the sedge my bones, and the grass my trampled hair."

Her strokes grew fainter and fainter, until at last the quiet waters closed over her,

AT LAST AINO FOUND HERSELF AT THE BORDER OF A WIDE LAKE

and even her long brown hair, floating behind, was lost as if she had never been.

Now who would take the news of little Aino back to her home where her mother was waiting?

The bear, the old man of the woods, waddled by and saw her scarlet ribbons on the pebbles, and he meant to take the sad, sad news, but he forgot, and ran among the sheep.

The wolf slank by like a gray ghost, and saw her sky-blue robe on the willow, and he meant to take the sad, sad news, but he forgot, and strayed among the cattle.

The fox flashed by, and saw her empty shoes, and he meant to tell the sad, sad tale, but he forgot, and frightened the geese.

"I will not forget," said the long-eared hare, with his mouth like a cross, as he sniffed at her golden belt on the sand. Then he bounded off on his crooked legs to tell the mournful story.

When he came to her home, he found her mother and the maids laughing and singing

[49]

in the bath-house, and switching each other with the whisks.

"Come here, Round Eye," called the mother, gaily, "and I will catch you and roast you for my daughter's dinner."

"Never," said the hare, boldly," for your daughter lies beneath the lake forever and forever, and the fishes are her only playmates."

The mother let her bath whisk fall, and sank back against the doorway.

"What have I done to my child?" she sobbed, "How have I cared for my little dove? I meant to marry her well, but I forced her into her grave!"

Her tears flowed down her robe, and over her stockings of scarlet wool and her gold embroidered shoes. Three mighty rivers sprang from the tears of Aino's mother, and they flowed by day and by night. In each great river was a waterfall, at the height of each waterfall a rock, on each rock there sprang a birch tree, and in each birch there sang a golden cuckoo.

"Darling, darling!" sang the first. Three months he sang for the little maid who lay beneath the waters before she had known love.

"Lover, lover!" sang the second. Six months he sang for the sad old wooer, who grieved for little Aino.

"Gladness, gladness!" sang the third, but he sang all his life for the mother whose tears would never cease.

"Why should the cuckoo call of youth and joy to a mother whose child is dead? For me there is no spring. My heart is failing and my life is shortened, when I hear the cuckoo call."

III

Vaino heard of the death of his darling, and all the night through he wept for the plump and rosy maiden over whose head the waters had closed forever. With the dawn he rose, and went to the edge of the lake to call on Untamo, the dreamer, the sage who has slept since before the world began, and in whose dreams all things exist.

"Untamo, Untamo, where shall I find the realm of Ahto, ruler of the misty sea, for one has gone there whom I am prone to follow."

Untamo stirred in his endless sleep, and out of his dreams his voice made answer.

"Near the headland, ever clouded,
Neath the isle in mist enshrouded,
Roofed in by the moving sea,
Will Ahto's coral palace be."

Vaino hurried to his boat, made ready his fishing tackle, and set out for the clouded headland, and the mist enshrouded isle. His copper rod quivered, his silver line sang as it flashed through the air, and dropped the golden hook in the water.

Day after day, Vaino rowed about the headland, casting his line, and in the nights he gave himself no sleep, but sat brooding over the quiet sea. One early morning, when the faint wind of dawn had just begun to ripple, the copper rod bent in his hand, the silver line tightened.

Vaino reeled it in, and took from the hook

a strange, strange fish. It was larger than a salmon, and pinker than a trout, smoother than a powan, and fairer than a pike. It was not a water nymph, for it wore no belt, and it was not a mermaid, for it had no long green hair.

"Whatever it is," said Vaino, "it must come from the deep, deep sea, and whatever it is, it is in time to be my breakfast."

He drew his silver case knife from its sheath, and made ready to hack the strange fish into pieces suitable for breakfast, lunch and dinner. But as he bent over it, the fish leapt from the boat's red floor, and slipped over the side into the water. It swam around and around him, and cried out:

"It was not to be eaten at breakfast that I came to thee, Vaino. It was not to be eaten at lunch, nor at dinner either."

"Why did you come, strange fish?" asked Vaino.

The strange fish reared itself up out of the water, and showed him the merry little face of Aino, her plump brown shoulders, and her dimpled hands.

"Silly old man," she said, "I would have nestled beside you like a round little dove, and I would have been your loving wife, to sit on your knee and make your bed, sweep the room, light the fire, bake the bread, make the honey cakes, and fill your tankard with beer. But you did not know me. You could not hold me. All your years have not taught you how to hold me. And now, farewell, farewell forever, for I must go to the dark and misty halls of Ahto."

With a last wave of her hand, she turned her round brown body, and dived deep into the water. Vaino leaned over the side of the boat, and saw her vanish into a crevice in the rocks, far, far beneath him.

"Return, return, Aino!" he cried with his heart in his voice, but she never came back to him. He never saw her again.

Vaino wove a silken net, and trolled it over many waters, catching every sort of fish in the lakes and the sea, but never again did he catch Aino.

Vaino beat his breast, and called himself a fool, and cursed his lack of understanding, but never again did he see Aino.

Vaino made a lament, for his loneliness and his folly, and the path which he must tread with no one beside him, saying,

"Grief has stilled the singing of the
    birds,
The cuckoo no longer sings for the
    sunrise."

"I wish that my mother were living," cried Vaino in his sorrow. "She would help me. With my whole heart I long for my mother. She would teach me how to bear my grief."

Far down under the white-topped waves his mother heard him, and stirred in her grave. Even dead mothers waken when their children cry.

"Do not mourn, my son, my little Vaino.

Do not mourn for that girl. There is no maiden living worth a tear from your eye. In Pohja, the uttermost northland, there are fairer and fatter maids by the score."

Vaino heard her, and in time he ceased his sighing.

———

Fru Lundborg finished speaking and folded her work in her lap.

"It is so sad!" cried young Vaino. "Mother, why is it so sad?"

"What do you do in the summer, my son?" asked his mother.

"I play in the fields, and practise my running."

"And what do you do in the winter?"

"I go to school and study my lessons."

"You see," said Fru Lundborg, "in the summer, in the time of joy, you are gay, but in the winter, in the cold and the darkness, you learn to be a man. It has been winter in the hearts of the Finnish people for long

[56]

years, and they have made their strength from their sorrow."

For a little while after that they were silent, and Vaino went on with his carving, making himself a pair of wooden shoes with which to stamp about in the spring mud. Fru Lundborg got up to light the lamp.

Suddenly, without warning, they heard the front door slam, there was a heavy foot in the hall, then the door of the quiet room burst open and a man sprang in, slammed it, and fell back against it, panting.

He was hatless, his boots and the skirts of his coat were covered with snow, his face was ghastly. Fru Lundborg moved so that she stood between him and Vaino, who, speechless with astonishment, looking over her shoulder, saw that it was the Russian officer of that unforgettable afternoon on the road.

"Hide me!" gasped the man, as if he had barely the breath for those two words.

"Are they close behind you?" asked Fru Lundborg.

"They shot my horse. I got away in the woods. Threw them off. Must hide!"

Fru Lundborg answered him in a stolid measured voice. "I have no reason to love the Russians."

The officer sagged back against the door. He said nothing, but there was a terrible pleading in his eyes. Vaino noticed that his sword belt was gone, and thought that he must have thrown it away to lighten himself. The mother spoke again.

"Have you left tracks in the snow outside the door?"

"I ran the last half mile in the trodden road. I can't run any more."

"You can't stay here. Think of the danger to my family if you were found. Besides, I am your enemy."

"I'm finished," said the Russian in a despairing whisper. He leaned against the door as if he had lost the power of motion, and his coat hung loose like a scarecrow's rags from his drooping shoulders. Vaino expected to see him crumple up and fall forward on the floor at any minute.

"You must go," answered Fru Lundborg implacably.

When the man did not move, she turned her back on him, opened the door of the stove, and threw in a chunk of wood. Then she added, absent-mindedly, as if to herself, "But this is a large house. I do not go into every room of it every day." She faced him again, with a long level stare.

The officer looked at her, and his eyes widened. He almost smiled. With a tremendous effort he straightened himself up and started to open the door.

"Wait!" called Fru Lundborg, and the man turned his head toward her, agonized, as a drowning man might look at land. "My son Sven has some old clothes upstairs."

The Russian nodded, closed the door behind him softly, and the room was as quiet as if he had never been there.

"Mother," cried Vaino, "that was the man

I met on the road! What is he going to do?"

"How should I know? We must try to forget him. Come, bring out your accordion, and let's sing a song together."

While Vaino was getting the accordion from its corner, his mother took a cloth and wiped up a pool of melted snow by the doorway. Then she lit the lamp, left the window blind up so that anyone could see in, and sat down again to her sewing. Soon they were singing together merrily, her rich deep voice blending with his clear soprano. It was in the middle of the second song that they heard a blowing of automobile horns outside, but she made a little sign that they should pay no attention, so they went on singing. Then there was a thundering at the door, and a lot of shouting. Outside in the half dusk, Vaino could see the lights of two cars, and many men running up to the house.

"Wait here by the fire," said Fru Lundborg, "and remember to let me do the talking." She crossed the hall and opened the front door. "What do you want?" she asked in Finnish.

It sounded as though they were all trying to answer at once, and then they started to push past her into the house, but she was too quick for them. She was still between them and Vaino as they surged into the living room, and they stopped, slightly abashed, by the door. They were about a dozen, six or seven Russian soldiers, and five or six Finnish workmen, and they exhaled a strong smell of aquavit, and waved some pistols loosely. They had been exchanging caps with one another until none of them had head-gear which fitted. The Finns seemed to be the leaders. One of them had tied a red hand-kerchief about his arm. One of the Russians had an officer's sword, which he shook in the air.

Fru Lundborg faced them, her broad shoulders squared back, her head up. Behind her Vaino sat by the stove, with the accordion still in his lap. She spoke in Finnish.

"I don't know what you have done with

your manners, the whole lot of you, shoving yourselves into people's houses like this. If one of you will speak at a time, I will try to answer you."

There was a little mumbling and shoving among them, then the workman with the red handkerchief was pushed forward, and explained in a slightly thickened tongue that they had traced a Russian officer through the woods to the road which ran past her house, and that they thought he might be hiding here, and they demanded him in the name of Finland, and of the People, and of Freedom, and of the Workers, and of Justice.

Fru Lundborg put her hands on her hips and stared at them. "What on earth would a Finnish woman like me be doing with a Russian officer?"

Somebody muttered "bourgeoise," another "traitor," and the shouting began again. Fru Lundborg shook her fists in the air over her head, and shouted louder than any of them.

"Look here, Finns! I have nothing to say

to you Russians. I'm a Finn too, a pure Finn. My dead husband may have had a Swedish name, but he was as good a Finn as any of you. I speak your language, and I have a Finnish heart. I'm ashamed of you. Have you nothing better to do for your country than to drink too much vodka, chase one man through the woods, and come and insult your countrywomen? The road which runs to my house runs past my house, so let me hear no more about it."

For a moment she had silenced them. The Finns in the party looked shamefacedly at the floor, but they did not go, and the Russians, most of whom spoke a little Finnish, began whispering. Fru Lundborg smiled, a wide, generous smile which took them all in, and stretched out her hand to them.

"Come along, friends, get warm before you start back to town. Vaino, tune up and play them that song again. The one we were singing when they came. They are no true Finns if they don't know it too!"

Vaino, who had never let go of the accordion, swung into a lively folksong. He played well, although Sven played better. His mother took up the tune in her rich full voice, beating time with her hands, and waving the men into the room. As the first Finn passed her she made a gesture of welcome such as they use in the peasant dances, and the man took off his cap. The others followed his example, and soon they were all roaring in chorus around the stove. The Russians could carry the tune although they did not know the words. When they finished the first song, they had a second and a third.

Then Fru Lundborg spoke again.

"Well, friends, I wish I could ask you to stay longer, but I have supper to get for myself and the boy. There's not food in the house for the lot of us, worse luck, or I would ask you to stay too. I know you will excuse me, for probably some of you are married, and you know how women are."

With a snatch of the last song, she mar-

shalled them to the door, and stood there,
with one arm around Vaino, waving to them
as they piled into the two automobiles. They
were still humming and laughing, they huz-
zahed, and waved their hats in the air, the
cars were hard to start, and that made them
laugh all the more. As they finally whirled
off, one of them caught two pistols from his
comrades, and fired both into the air, for
good measure.

When they were out of sight, Fru Lundborg shut the door, and went with Vaino
back to the fire. For a moment she closed her
eyes, and leaned on him so heavily that he
thought she was going to fall down, and he
put both arms around her tightly until she
looked at him, and smiled.

"You were a true Finn, son. I was proud
of you. Now you see that it is not only in the
old legends that songs are more than swords."
She put her hand on his head, and pressed it
against her breast. "Come along to the
kitchen. It is time we had something to eat."

"Let's have it here," said Vaino, when she had finished preparing the food. "It is such a bore to go into the dining room when there are only us two." Vaino liked the kitchen, with its white wooden floor which was scoured with sand every day, and the rows of copper pots and pans which shone like mirrors.

They were about to sit down when they heard footsteps in the corridor, and a very odd figure of a man appeared in the door, looking so funny that Vaino nearly laughed aloud. He was wearing Sven's oldest overcoat, much too short in the sleeves, and much too broad in the shoulders, a pair of baggy trousers, also too short, old shoes which slipped about on his feet, and a fur cap which the moths had eaten, that perched lightly on Sven's broad head, but came down over this man's ears. His moustache was gone, but he was still the Russian officer.

He pulled off his cap when he came into the kitchen, and took a purse from his pocket.

He was no longer the stricken, hunted creature who had come in an hour ago, but neither was he the self-assured bully whom
Vaino had met on the road. With his purse in
hand, he looked at Fru Lundborg, and something in her eyes bade him put it back in his
pocket.

"Which way are you going?" she asked.

"I don't know."

"I advise you to try it over the ice to
Sweden. There is a man called Haapi in Abo
who will help you if you come from me. My
name is Lundborg.

The Russian came nearer, and held out
his hand.

"How can I thank you, Madame?"

Fru Lundborg clasped her hands behind
her, and did not move. "We are all human
beings I suppose. You had better take this."
She picked up the loaf of black bread from
the table and handed it to him. He put it in
his pocket. Then he bowed from the waist,
very low, as if he were bowing to an empress,

and jerking himself up, saluted stiffly. Fru
Lundborg opened the door, and the darkness
outside swallowed him up.

"Come, child," she said to Vaino, "eat
your thick pea soup before it gets cold. The
sooner you finish the sooner you can have
your clabber."

3

From Under the Sea

NEVER as long as he lived would Vaino forget the summer which followed—a summer of vague threats, whispered conferences, stories of outrage and atrocity, a summer of waning hope, and slowly mounting fear. It seemed that Finland was not to be free very soon, after all. Instead of withdrawing her soldiers, Russia sent more, and their behaviour grew wilder and wilder, but now one did not complain of "the Russians." It was "the Reds" who were the enemy, and that was worse, for they were Finns, Finnish workmen, speaking the mother tongue, nourished by the same Suomi.

Sven stayed in town for days at a time, and when he was at home, either alone or with friends, he was always sad, always preoccupied. Anniki too was away, except for rare visits, studying nursing, she said. As for Fru Lundborg, Vaino had never seen her so busy. She and Marta, the old maid of all work, were up every morning not many hours after sunrise (and the sun rises before three during a Finnish summer), spending the day in cooking, and sewing and weaving. They prepared for the coming winter as if there were never to be another spring, Vaino thought. Innumerable pounds of cheese, innumerable crocks of salted fish, and beans, and meat, were packed away in the dark, cool storehouse. Innumerable socks, and sweaters, and scarves were knitted for Sven and his friends, and his friends' friends.

On one dreadful, unforgettable evening, at

about ten o'clock, they were all sitting together in the garden, Sven was reading his newspaper in the clear, gray light, Fru Lundborg was knitting. Anniki had let down the two braids of her hair to rest her head, and they hung dark and straight on either side of her, almost touching the ground as she sat idle in her chair. She was not like herself in those days, very moody, very dreamy, very restless. Fru Lundborg watched her, but never scolded.

A fisherman, who lived farther down the road, came by with a letter which he had found at the village postoffice. Anniki always behaved as if every letter that came must be for her, but this one was for the mother, who when she read it, gave a little cry, and sat staring ahead of her with her hands clenched in her lap.

When they asked her what was the matter, "Your cousin Kullervo has been killed in Tammerfors," she said.

She sent Vaino to the house for an extra

ball of wool, and as he came back, he heard her saying, "the Reds came up to the room where he had taken refuge with the rest of his family, and called him out. 'We will bring him back, your husband!' one of them said, and laughed. And then later, when they threw him into the room again, they shouted, 'Here he is!' "

Her voice was trembling with indignation and sorrow.

It was after that that Anniki gave up her nursing, and began to come and go more mysteriously than ever. After that Vaino was not allowed to go to Helsingfors alone, for Sven had asked him to stay and look after their mother. That was all right, except that he was expected to practise his running in their own fields instead of making expeditions into the woods, and as he had to run at least five kilos every day, just trotting around and around grew very monotonous.

The only real fun he had that summer was going out in the little motor boat which he

and Sven had bought the year before. All
Finns are amphibious, and he learned to handle it very well alone. No one objected to
that, so long as he did not go out of sight of
shore.

In October the situation grew worse.
There were strikes and riots in Finland
nearly every day, and no one could do anything about it. In November the provisional
government was overthrown in Russia, but
that seemed to make no difference in Finland. The Reds began to break open the jails,
and let out all the criminals to join the Red
Guard.

"Why don't the police stop them?" asked
Vaino.

"There are no police now," said Sven,
"only the Red Guard. They can get all the
rifles and ammunition they need from the
Russians. We have just twenty guns for two
hundred men, we Whites, in Helsingfors.
You are old enough to know that you can't
fight armed men with your bare fists."

[73]

One day in the middle of November, Anniki came home in a state of exaltation. After she had talked to Fru Lundborg they called in Vaino.

"Listen, Vaino. You can help us, but of course you are never to say a word about this. Tonight there is coming a sending of arms and ammunition for us in a U-boat from Germany. We have expected it before, but now it is really here. Tonight it will come up in the Bay after dark, and flash three white lights and a red. The lighthouse on the island off shore will answer with five whites. Then seven motorboats are to go out from different places to unload it. I want you to take a man and me out in yours."

Vaino's heart nearly burst with joy and excitement, but he managed to be very dignified in his answer.

That afternoon he took a trial spin to see that the boat was in good shape, but he was very careful not to seem to be giving it undue attention. In the evening he could hardly eat his supper until his mother reminded him that it was important for him to keep up his strength.

As they left the house that night, Anniki caught her mother in her arms. "Do you forgive me for taking him, Mother?"

"You know how I feel," answered Fru Lundborg, smiling. Then she kissed Vaino again. "Remember, son, nothing is too much to give for Finland."

Their own woodland ran nearly to the water's edge. It was dark, and darker still among the trees, so that Vaino started when the black shape of a man loomed up beside them.

"Who is that?" asked Anniki, quietly.

"John Golden."

No one spoke again until they had stepped into the boat. It was a cold night, but the Bay had not yet frozen, although there was a thin skim of ice near the shore. Vaino was glad that his mother had made him wear his fur cap and pull it down over his ears. They pushed the boat out with the oars, and did not start the motor until the shore lights were yellow dots on the steel black edge of the sky.

Anniki broke the silence. "This is John Golden. I am Voima. There is no Anniki this evening."

Vaino thought that over. It seemed to him that as a fellow conspirator he ought to have a war name too. After a little while he said, "I am Kuervo Paali."

He was afraid that they might smile at him, but though it was too dark to see their faces there was no smile in their voices when they answered. After that they talked every now and then, calling each other by their new names, but most of the time they were silent. When they had gone quite a way out, they shut down the motor and drifted.

Black sky and black water melted together in indefinable space. Occasionally the lighthouse on the island behind them shot a white path along the glassy surface. There was nothing else to see, nothing to hear. They sat in the boat, and the dampness of the raw thin air crawled through their clothing.

At last, at long last, a white light glowed momentarily in the indistinguishable darkness, then another, and another, and then a red spark.

"There they are!" whispered Voima, hoarsely.

It was about nine thirty. The lighthouse answered with five white flashes, and Vaino steered his boat toward the spot where the lights had been.

When they had gone a little way in the empty darkness, suddenly they could see the U-boat before them. It lay low on the water, this mysterious monster from the bottom of the sea, a lightless hulk, beyond the reach of beams from any of the lighthouses. No sound came from it, but there in the open Bay the air throbbed faintly with the chugging of approaching motorboats.

One by one they took shape out of the

darkness, and as they shut down their motors, and drifted silently up to the submarine, they could see a row of black figures, standing along her rail.

Vaino's boat was the smallest there. It took all three of them to look after it, and do what was necessary, but some of the people from the larger boats went on board and were warmly welcomed. They had brought presents for the submarine's crew, a cheese of giant proportions, pounds and pounds of butter, one hundred cigars, and a keg of fine old brandy, greeted with cheers.

The young captain leaned over the side to talk with John Golden.

"We had an exciting trip out," he said, "Just below Hango we collided with a Russian submarine net, which we had to dive under, and a little farther we had a run-in with a chaser, but managed to get away."

At last all the motorboats were loaded and ready to go. Vaino had a cargo of two hundred kilograms of hand grenades, twenty-

five Mausers, and, best of all, one of the two
much needed and eagerly awaited wireless
receiving sets which the Germans had
brought. In farewell, the crew of the submarine lined up on deck, waved their caps
against the lowering sky, and gave a subdued
but hearty cheer for Finland. Then they
slipped away into the enveloping darkness.

One by one the other boats vanished also.
Soon "John," "Voima," and "Kuervo" were
alone in the empty meeting of sky and sea,
without lights, with the motor throttled down
to its most silent, nosing a cautious way into
shore. If Vaino had not known his little inlet
as he knew the fingers of his hand, he could
never have steered so straight into it, like a
homing bird, and glided the last stretch on
his momentum, so that they landed without
a sound.

They made the boat fast, and began un-
loading. John Golden had a Ford at a little
distance, into which they put the hand grenades, to be be driven back to the Helsingfors

that night. The Mausers they hid in a hollow tree, where Anniki had once made her doll's house. John lifted out the precious wireless set, and held it in his arms, while "Voima" and "Kuervo" groped over the boat to make sure that nothing had been left for the tell-tale daylight to reveal. Then they took it from him, and carrying it between them set out for the house. John Golden faded into the blackness between the trees.

The set was heavy, the ground filled with invisible roots and holes. A fine, ice-like rain began to fall and made everything slippery. They stumbled to the house as quickly as they could without making a noise, resting now and then. It was nearly three o'clock.

Vaino's eyes felt as if he had rubbed sand in them, his back and arms ached from the heavy packages he had been handling, he was wet through, chilled through, and prouder and happier than he had ever been in his life.

No lights showed in the silent house as

they toiled up to it, but they found the
kitchen door open as had been arranged, and
a voice came to them out of the darkness inside. "Children?"

"It's all right, Mother," answered Anniki.

They sat the wireless apparatus down on
the kitchen table, while Fru Lundborg shut
and bolted the door. She had an electric torch
in her hand.

"The curtains are drawn," she said, "but
I don't want to make a light here at this time
of night. There is coffee on the stove. Put
plenty of hot milk in yours, Vaino, so that it
will not keep you awake. You must both be
sopping wet. Take off your clothes right
away, and we will leave them to dry over-
night. I've warmed your beds. What is this
thing on the table?"

Anniki explained. "Thank heaven it won't
explode!" said Fru Lundborg. While they
drank their coffee and ate some sandwiches
she took the set, lifting it easily, and hid it

[81]

in one of the capacious kitchen cupboards.

The coffee did not keep Vaino awake. To this day he has no memory of getting to bed that night, only a vague impression of someone large and soft, probably his mother, bending over him.

When he woke up next morning it was after ten o'clock and Anniki, dressed for town, was sticking her head in his door.

"Hello there! How are you? You were a great kid last night."

She came over and patted his shoulder. She was dressed in the long gray cape of her nursing costume. Vaino stretched out a sleepy hand, and came into violent contact with something hard.

"Look out," she said, "I've got several Mausers bestowed about me, so don't barge into them like that. It hurts. Let me tell you what is going to happen. Tomorrow there will be a parade at your school. You and I will drive in to meet the others in our own pony cart, all decorated to represent the king and queen of winter. After the parade I will take you to a certain house. We will spread the white bearskin to sit on in the cart, and what do you think will be under the bearskin? The wireless, of course!"

By this time Vaino was wide awake, and jumped out of bed in delight, eager to trim the cart at once. Fru Lundborg came in and sat on the edge of his bed.

"This is a holiday for you, child. You don't have to go to school until tomorrow. Anniki, here is a letter."

The letter had a German postmark. Anniki snatched at it, and read it feverishly.

"It is in our code," she said, "he tells me he is going to the Eastern front."

She was talking about Scarelius of course, thought Vaino. It was perfectly disgusting the way she always spoke of Scarelius as if he were the only man in the world.

Suddenly she crumpled the letter, and her face crumpled like the paper. Flinging herself on the floor with a great clatter of metal, she buried her head in her mother's lap.

"I'm so afraid, Mother! I'm so afraid!"

Her mother patted her shoulder, lifted off her hat, and smoothed her hair. "Of course you are, my darling, but you are not going to give way to it, because you have your work to do here."

In a minute or two Anniki pulled herself together. She got up, rearranged her load, put on her hat, and even managed to smile at them from the door, as she went out.

"Why was she afraid?" asked Vaino, who thought she had made rather an exhibition of herself.

"She is afraid that Scarelius may get killed in the fighting," answered Fru Lundborg; then, as she saw Vaino's face lengthen, she changed her tone, and added, lightly, "terrible things happen to Finns when they leave home. If you will come in by the stove where it is warm I will give you your breakfast, and tell you about it."

Vaino put on his fur slippers, and did as she suggested, and when she had provided him with a big bowl of porridge and a glass of milk, she began.

The Magic Mill

Vaino mounted his straw-colored pony, and set forth for Pohja. At an easy trot he ambled through the meadows of Suomi, with his white hair, and the yellow tail of the pony streaming behind in the breeze, and his blue-veined hand firm on the bridle reins. When they came to the edge of the sea the pony did not check his pace, but trotted ahead, up one side of the heaving billows and down the other, without even wetting his neat little hooves.

The air was clear and cool above the water, and Vaino let it blow through his beard as he ambled along, wrapped in his blue cloak, mounted on his wheat-yellow pony, up and down over the moving waves.

To reach Pohja, the Uttermost North-land, Vaino must ride past the coasts of Lapland, where Jouka still dwelt, nourishing still a hope for revenge, and a hatred blacker than a serpent's blood. Thinking all the while of his lost sister, Aino, Jouka had made a crossbow of iron, inlaid with copper and silver and gold. A running horse adorned the stock, a sleeping woman rounded the curve, a hare crouched at the catch, and the strings were sinews from the elk of Hiisi, the land of evil. He made arrows of oak and pine, feathered them with swallow tails, and dipped the points in the venom of an adder.

The window of Jouka's workroom looked on the sea, and every morning, every evening, every noontime, Jouka sat there, waiting and watching. His narrow black eyes did not tire, nor his hand loosen on the crossbow. Sometimes he stood on the step, sometimes he walked down into the meadow, always waiting, always watching.

Early one morning, as he stood on the

farthest and strangest tongue of land, where the waterfall plunged to the sea, he saw in the distance a dark speck, a speck that lightened into blue.

"Is it a cloud?" asked Jouka. All the time he knew it was no cloud, but Vaino, ambling along on his wheaten-yellow pony. He drew an arrow, and fitted it to his string.

"What are you doing, son?" cried his mother, hurrying up behind him.

"Getting ready to shoot old Vaino through the liver," snarled Jouka without turning.

"Son, son," exclaimed his mother in great agitation, "you mustn't do that. Song and joy will perish from the world with Vaino. They will follow him to Tuonela, the Land of the Dead."

For a moment Jouka hesitated. Then he shouted, "What do I care!" and loosed his arrow.

It flew too high. He drew again and shot, but the arrow flew too low. A third time he shot, and the hissing arrow sank deep into the heart of the wheaten-yellow pony.

The pony fell, and Vaino rolled from its back into the water, clutching at it with his fingers. Then a great wind and a great wave bore him out into the open sea.

Jouka sang in triumph, in spite of the fact that his mother reproved him.

"Twang my crossbow! Sing my arrow!
Farewell, Vaino, and forever!
May you never tread your homeland,
May you never see the sunshine,
May you toss about forever
Like a dead log in the water."

For nine days, Vaino tossed over the open sea, under the open sky, helpless, cold, and suffering. At last the sky above him was darkened by an eagle. Although it was neither the largest nor the smallest of the eagles, one wing swept the water, while the other swept the heaven. It hovered over Vaino, and asked him how he came in such wretched plight.

"Alas," said Vaino, telling what had happened, "I do not know whether I shall die by drowning or starvation."

"It shall be neither," answered the eagle, "for I have not forgotten how in that day when you felled the forests and cleared the fields of Suomi, you left the birch for the birds to rest in, and especially for me. Climb on my back, stand between my wings, and I will carry you wherever you like."

Then Vaino mounted on the wings of the eagle, and soaring down the path of the East Wind, alighted on the dim and misty shores of Pohja, the Uttermost Northland.

When the eagle left him, he stood alone on the shore, wounded, weary, his beard tangled by a thousand winds, his robe stained by a thousand seas. The ocean behind him was not more trackless than the bare strange land before him, and Vaino thought of home, and filled the air with loud laments.

Now the Maid of Pohja had promised the sun that she would always rise before him, to clip the sheep, and card the wool, and weave it on her loom. So early on this morn-- ing she had washed the table, and swept the floor, and carried the sweepings from her broom of twigs out to the farthest field. There she heard a sound of weeping from across the bay.

She ran home with the news to her mother, Louhi, Mistress of Pohja. Louhi, the bent and wrinkled crone, blew through her three remaining teeth, then leaning on her stick hurried down to the fence corner, and twisted her withered neck to listen.

"It is neither a child nor a woman," she said, "but a strong man weeping across the bay."

Gathering her petticoats, she jumped into her boat, and taking the oars in her knotted hands, she rowed over to the barren shore where there grew only a few clumps of wil- low, and a tangled hedge of cherry. There stood Vaino. His mouth was quivering, and his beard was shaking, but he did not open his lips to speak to her.

"I see you are a stranger," said the Mistress of Pohja.

"Indeed I am a stranger," answered Vaino, "this is a foreign land to me, and I was better off in my own country."

"What is your noble race, and what your heroic lineage?" asked Louhi politely.

"Once I bore a name that was famous, once I met evening cheerfully, singing in the valleys of Suomi. Now my grief is so great that I do not know who I am."

Louhi then became very practical. She coaxed him into her boat by expressing a longing to hear all about his adventures, and rowed him over to her house. There she fed him, warmed him, and rubbed his stiffened limbs before she asked any more questions.

"My life is too short for the tears I must weep," said Vaino, when he had been made perfectly comfortable, "since I have strayed so far from my beloved homeland. Your doors and your gates are strange to me, even your trees are unfriendly to me. The pine twigs scratch me, the birches flog me, the alders stab me. Only the shining sun and the kindly wind are as I have known them."

"You will be well off here, Vaino," said Louhi encouragingly. "See, I have both salmon and pork on the table. Draw up and take whatever you like."

"The best of food is not good in a stranger's house. Water from a mudhole at home is better than mead in golden goblets abroad. A man is better off at home. Jumala, Creator, grant that I may see my home again."

Artful old Louhi showed all three of her teeth in a cunning smile, and hitched herself nearer on her three-legged stool.

"What will you give me, Vaino, if I send you back to the edge of your own wheat fields?"

"Whatever you like, if only I may hear my own birds sing again, and my cuckoo call.

Shall it be a hat full of gold, or a helmet full of silver?"

"Gold is a child's toy, and silver we melt into bells to hang on our horses. I would have you forge me a Sampo, a magic mill which will grind out prosperity and happiness. These are the ingredients,

> One white grain of barley,
> White wing-tip of swan,
> Milk of virgin heifer,
> Wool of ewe, new shorn.

If you will forge me a Sampo, you shall have my daughter for your wife, and your own birds shall sing about you, in the trees of your own land.

"Alas, I can forge nothing," answered Vaino, "but if you will let me go I will bring you Ilmarinen the Smith. It was he who wrought out the dome of heaven so cunningly that not a hammer mark can be seen on it, and forged the foundations of the air. Undoubtedly he could make a Sampo, and win the maiden too."

Louhi had to be satisfied with this, so she led out her milk-white stallion, and yoked him to a sledge for Vaino. As he set forth she gave him a last warning not to look to the right nor to the left, nor above him nor behind, lest it should be the worse for him.

At the edge of the misty land of Pohja Vaino drove beneath the arch of the rainbow. On it sat the Maid of Pohja, clad in robes of shining white, weaving a fabric of gold and silver with a golden shuttle on a silver loom.

When Vaino heard the shuttle humming above him he forgot the warning, and looked up, and that was an evil day for Vaino, for afterward he wished the maiden for himself.

He did not tarry then, however, but drove home at tremendous speed. The runners of his sledge rang over the wide heaths, through the swamps, across the meadows. His heart was bursting with joy when at last he came to the long road leading to Suomi, with the mist of brown hemlock twigs on either side, and the flat green branches overhead.

How Vaino sang in his own land! How he called on the wolves to devour those who had tried to keep him away from it! How he rejoiced over every stone in the road!"

"I must make something with my songs," said Vaino to himself, and added as an afterthought, "I must make something useful," for Vaino remembered that he must send Imarinen the Smith to Pohja, and knew that it might not be easy.

He paused in the last meadow before he reached his house. The white-maned stallion was glad to stand grazing, knee-deep in the long grass, grateful that his soft nose no longer sniffed the hard brown earth of Pohja. Standing in the sledge with his feet apart, and his travel-stained cloak thrown wide, Vaino sang.

A small birch in the meadow began to grow. The song rose and swelled, and the birch tree topped the trees of the wood which ringed the meadow. Vaino sang more loudly, and the top of the birch swept the sky. Vaino waved his arm in a circle, and the melody of his song circled with his arm. The birch tree burst into flower at the top, one of the flowers was the pale white moon, and the others were sparkling stars.

Satisfied with his magic, Vaino called to the stallion and drove on, with his hat pulled down over his eyes, thinking blackly of his promise to send the Smith to Pohja.

Soon he drew up at the door of the smithy, and a merry clang of iron came out to meet him. The smithy was built of logs, with moss growing green on the high roof, and gay sparks flying out of the open door. Inside, Ilmarinen, tall, bare to the waist, bent his reddened face over the fire, pushing back the damp, sooty hair which lay in curls on his forehead.

Ilmarinen knew no wonder-working songs, such as Vaino used. "These are my songs," he would say, laughing, and stretching out his two great fists, as supple as they were strong, with the muscles knotting under the smooth brown skin. A man of few words and simple heart was Ilmarinen.

He looked up from his work and saw Vaino climbing out of the sledge. He dropped his hammer and ran out, showing all of his strong white teeth in a smile, and shouting, "Vaino, Vaino, where have you been all this time?"

"I have been in the dark and gloomy land of Pohja, where the snow lies forever," answered Vaino. "There I ran on the strange snowshoes of the Lapps, and learned their ancient magic."

"However did you get there, and however did you get back?" asked Ilmarinen, taking the singer's blue-veined hand in his great brown one, and leading him to a bench beside the smithy door.

Vaino told him how he had been rescued by the eagle, and sent back kindly by the Mistress of Pohja herself. "But this is the best of it," he added, looking into Ilmarinen's wondering eyes, "there is a maiden in Pohja who rides upon the rainbow, and outshines the sun and the stars by the light of her beauty. She will wed only a man who can forge a Sampo, and when I heard that I hurried home to tell you about it, for you are surely the one man in the world who could win this peerless bride."

"Not me!" said Ilmarinen, starting up hastily. "I'll never go to that fearful country. I have even heard that they eat each other there, when winter closes in."

"I should go if I were you," answered Vaino. "Her eyes gleam like the moon, and the sunshine itself streams from her flowing hair."

"Not for twenty girls," cried Ilmarinen. Then he grew suspicious. "Did you promise to send me so that they would let you go?"

Vaino smiled soothingly. "If you do not trust me we must talk of something else. On my way home I passed a wonderful tree, the

ILMARINEN LOOKED UP FROM HIS WORK AND SAW VAINO CLIMBING OUT OF THE
SLEDGE

top of which sweeps the sky, and the flowers of it are the moon and the stars."

"I'd have to see that to believe it," answered Ilmarinen, with a good-natured laugh.

"Come along then!" cried Vaino, and he led Ilmarinen to the meadow where the tree was growing, straight and tall, with its flowery crown of stars brushing the sky, and the moon the final glory.

Vaino sighed. "If I had strong young arms, and strong young legs, I should climb the tree, and bring down the moon and the stars for my people of Suomi."

"I could do it," said Ilmarinen, doubtfully, when he had recovered from his astonishment.

"You? Why you would be afraid to climb so high."

"No I wouldn't." Ilmarinen hitched up his belt, and striding to the tree began to climb.

As he swung himself up with his mighty

arms, higher and higher into the daylight, the branches beneath him groaned, "Beware! Beware!"

"Why?" asked Ilmarinen.

"False moon, false stars," groaned the branches, but Ilmarinen was not to be dissuaded by a tree, and climbed steadily up.

On the ground below, Vaino began to sing. Wild and terrible was his song, and a wild wind rose with it. The wind screamed through the wood, whipping Vaino's beard furiously about his head, and Vaino clung to his cloak and bent before it shouting, "Take him to Pohja! Take him to Pohja!"

The wind howled through the top of the trees, and tore Ilmarinen from the branches to which he was clinging with all his strength. Tossed to and fro, whirled round and round, over the moon and under the sun, sailed Ilmarinen in the fierce ship of the wind. For one moment he bestrode the shoulders of the Great Bear. Then at last he dropped into the courtyard of Pohja's hall,

and the storm was silent as suddenly as it had risen.

Not a watchdog barked at the stranger. Inside old Louhi listened to the silence, then hurried to the door. There stood Ilmarinen, feet apart, head up, and white teeth shining.

"How did you pass the watch-dogs?" asked Louhi.

"I've not come all this way to be barked at!" cried Ilmarinen, shouting for joy at having firm earth under his feet again.

Then Louhi understood the manner of his coming. "Tell me, you who ride the ship of the wind, and the sledge of the storm, did you meet Ilmarinen the master smith on your journey?"

"I am Ilmarinen, the Best Smith in the World!"

When she heard that, Louhi could not do enough for him. She brought him in, gave him a stool, and hurried to find the Maid of Pohja.

"Get up, daughter, put on your rainbow

gown, your brightest beads. See that your face is rosy, and wear your sweetest smile. Smith Ilmarinen, who will forge us a Sampo if he likes you, is here."

The Maid of Pohja bound her rainbow gown with a golden girdle, and fastened her white veil with a wreath of copper. Her silver earrings tinkled as she walked. Never was maid more beautiful than she, as she served Ilmarinen to food and drink. When her hand touched his, and she turned her rosy face bashfully away, Ilmarinen's heart leapt within him as it had never leapt before.

Louhi kept her shrewd little eyes fixed on his face, and after he was warmed and fed and rested, she said, "You may have her, Ilmarinen, if you will only make us one little Sampo."

"What of?" asked Ilmarinen.

"One white grain of barley,
  White wing-tip of swan,
  Milk of virgin heifer,
  Wool of ewe, new shorn."

"That sounds easy," said Ilmarinen, neg-
ligently, with his eyes on the maiden, "for
a man who has forged the dome of the sky."

Next day he sought a place for his smithy.
He had no tools, no bellows, no anvil, no
hammer, only a great wish to succeed since
he had seen the Maid of Pohja.

"Only old women despair, only rascals
leave work half done." he kept saying to
himself, as he painstakingly made the necessary equipment. When all was ready, Louhi
gave him servants to work the bellows, and
for three days they pumped away, using all
their strength. Then Ilmarinen stooped and
looked into the fire.

Out of the flame rose a golden crossbow
tipped with silver. But the bow was evil. It
demanded a head every day, and two on holy
days. Ilmarinen could not like it, so he broke
it up and cast it back into the fire.

For several days the servants blew harder
than ever. Ilmarinen looked into the flames,

[103]

and out of them rose a red boat with a golden prow. But the boat was evil. It would go to war whether it had a reason or not. Ilmarinen could not like it, so he broke it up and cast it back into the fire.

Then the servants pumped with might and main. Ilmarinen looked into the fire, and drew out a golden plowshare. But the plow was evil. It plowed up the cornfields and the grazing grounds. Ilmarinen could not like it, so he broke it up, and cast it back into the flames.

"This must be the home of evil itself," he said, "or else I shall never get anywhere with these lazy servants." But he decided to try them once more.

They blew and they blew, while he urged them on, until they fell down exhausted by the furnace. Then he drew out of the fire a young heifer with golden horns. But the heifer was evil. She wasted her milk in the forest. Ilmarinen could not like her, so he broke her up and cast her back into the fire.

"Be off with you!" he roared at the servants, and they ran. "Now I shall get some real help!"

In a lusty voice he called to the winds, called them by name, as a man might call his horses in a field, and the East, West, North, and South winds answered to his call. They blew furiously, one day—two days—three days. The fire flashed from the windows, the sparks flew from the door, the smoke clouded heaven. On the evening of the third day, Ilmarinen peered into the bottom of the furnace, and saw the Sampo forming into shape.

He seized it with his tongs, raised it out, and hammered at the many colored cover, where the silver and copper and gold ran together. All night he hammered, exulting in his strength, and as he worked a song came to him, came to him the songless, and he hammered its magic into the metal.

[105]

"By the light of the moon over which I
    have sailed,
By the light of my fire,
By the strength of the winds which
    before me have quailed,
By my own strength entire,
I weld the Sampo, where others have
    failed.
I weld heart's desire."

In the whispering dawn, Ilmarinen carried out the Sampo, and set it down before the door. It began to grind. As the pictured cover spun round and round, wheat streamed from one side of the mill, salt from another, and from another golden coins, clinking as they fell. Old Louhi came running at the grinding of the Sampo, and danced for joy until her gray skirts flapped about her bony ankles.

The Sampo ground all day. First enough for the people of dark and hungry Pohja to eat and be satisfied, then enough for them to trade for skins and knives and all they might require, then enough for them to store away against the ice-bound winter.

At evening Louhi caught it up in her skinny arms, and hugging it to her breast, carried it off to the Copper Mountain, where she locked it in with nine strong locks.

When she came back, Ilmarinen was ready for her.

"I've made the Sampo. How about the maiden?"

The Maid of Pohja shrank away from his brown hands.

"If I should leave my mother," she said, "the spring and the birds and the berries would vanish with me. Spring is in me, and not yet would I abandon dancing in the woods, and singing in the meadows."

Ilmarinen stared down at the floor, and pushed his cap onto the back of his sooty head. "Don't come if you don't want to," he muttered. Then he went out and sat down on a stone, and began to wonder sadly how he should ever get back to Suomi.

There old Louhi found him. "I expect you are thinking of your own land," she said cunningly, for now that she had used him she was anxious to get rid of him.

"I should at least like to die and be buried there," answered Ilmarinen with a sigh.

Then Louhi made all possible haste to lead him to a boat. She put food in it for him, she showed him how to paddle, she bade the North wind speed him, and as he drew away from the shore she grinned until she showed all three of the teeth in her withered gums.

At last Ilmarinen reached Suomi. In silence he went to the darkened doorway of his old forge. On the bench outside the door Vaino was sitting, sunning himself, and at sight of Ilmarinen he sprang up, and greeted him with outstretched hands.

"I knew all along that you would come back safely, brother Ilmarinen. Here I have been sitting waiting for you all this time. What a travelled hero you are now, to be sure! Tell me, did you forge the Sampo?

One white grain of barley,
White wing-tip of swan,
Milk of virgin heifer,
Wool of ewe new shorn.

That was the charm, wasn't it?"

"I forged the Sampo, all right," answered
Ilmarinen sadly. And walking past Vaino
into the disused smithy, he began to set it
to rights.

4

The Winter of Fear

THE winter of fear dragged on.
It was the time of year when the
ships freeze fast in the open bay,
and the passengers walk to shore if they can
get there, when the deep silent snow ac-
cumulates in strata, and obliterates the lakes
and brooks, when the languid sun, like a pale
balloon, rises at ten o'clock, describes a weary
arc on the horizon, and sinks again before
three. It was the time of year when noses
and ears must be watched if one is not to

lose them, when summer is a brief sweet legend, and a bright fire in a tall stove represents the highest hope of human comfort.

Finland declared herself independent on December fourth. It was announced in Vaino's school, and everyone cheered, but aside from that it seemed to make no difference. Russia recognized her, but sent two fresh trainloads of troops, and more arms to the Reds. Even their own leaders could no longer control the Red Guard. Sven laughed when he read their recruiting notices in their paper, "The Worker."

"Men wishing to join and defend the people against the bloodthirsty bourgeoisie must be members of the Social-Democratic party, and have class consciousness."

Toward the end of January events succeeded each other very quickly. Vaino was kept out of school again. The White President sent a manifesto to Russia, and Russia

sent renewed encouragement to the Reds.
The White government fled out of Helsingfors in the night, and took the gold reserve
with them. The Civil guard, including Sven,
went into hiding, or found refuge near
Borgo. They were hopelessly underarmed,
and outnumbered. The Reds seized the rail-
ways, the police, the telegraph and telephone, the newspapers, and set up their own
government.

It was WAR.

But it was not the long-awaited war
against a foreign enemy. It was Finn against
Finn, brother against brother, telling lies
about each other, and believing them, hating
each other, distrusting each other, fighting
each other. The new Russia was not content
with mere political supremacy. It reached
down to mould the very thoughts of the Finnish people.

The Whites had just one hope. Their general, Mannerheim, gathered his forces, attacked on the West coast, and telegraphed

that he had captured five thousand Russians, and set up his headquarters at Vasa.

Fru Lundborg and Vaino were alone at home. It was too dangerous for Sven to visit them from his camp. Anniki came and went on her mysterious errands. When things had been going on for about ten days, Fru Lundborg made up a package of chocolate, malt, brandy and cigarettes, for Vaino to take to Sven.

He was to plan to spend the night, as the camp was about a thirty-kilo run across country on skis. All the lakes were frozen of course, and the going was fairly good in spite of the woods. Although there were Reds scattered about, they were not likely to harm a boy, and the peasants were almost solidly with the Whites. Vaino had a bite of lunch at eleven, and started off, a knapsack on his back, his fur cap pulled down, and his muffler pulled up until only his eyes peered out between them. He kept up a good pace. The snow was ideal for skiing, so dry and fine that

[113]

it creaked under him. The sun on it made him blink and his body was warm inside his wrappings. There were plenty of down hills to rest him from the up hills, and there was extra chocolate in his pocket for him to nibble on when he felt hungry. The gradual dusk was beginning to gather when he knocked on the door of the school house which had been turned into a barrack.

He went in boldly, although his excitement was nearly choking him, and before his lips had time to frame a question his eyes had spotted Sven, in a far corner of the room, playing patience with another man. It did not take Vaino long to reach him.

Vaino was welcomed, and introduced all around, the package was opened, and the chocolate had disappeared among the corps before he had time to notice the other patience player. When he did his mouth fell open, and he nearly dropped the biscuit he was eating. This tall, slender young man with the black hair and the blue chin wore a uniform, which like the others looked as if it had been collected from a variety of warehouses, and had the white band on his arm, but his wild black eyes were unmistakable. It was the Russian Officer!

He threw back his head and laughed when he saw Vaino's astonishment.

"So you recognize me, little enemy? Sven, say a good word for me before he gives an alarm!"

While they sat down to the soldier's supper of the inevitable bean soup, sour bread, and milk, the Russian, who said that his only name for the present was Vladimir, told Vaino his story.

"When I left you and your charming mother, last March, I tried to get back to Russia. I reached Reval during the summer, and learned there that I had nothing to go home for. I came back to Finland, and while I was helping some Whites in Kotka the Reds got hold of me, and without due consideration very rudely decided to shoot me.

But they had no bullets with my name on them, so I got away, and a week ago I found your brother, and these other nice young men."

It was amazing, thought Vaino as he listened, how nice all kinds of people really were when you knew them. Vladimir had come into the camp still wearing Sven's overcoat, which Sven recognized, and so they had found out about each other. Now they were good friends because they had been such good enemies.

"Don't be uneasy," said Vladimir to Vaino, "I am just as glad to be fighting the Reds as your brother is, and for my own reasons."

"If you are not too tired, will speak only when you are spoken to, and take orders like a good soldier, you can come out with Vladimir and me tonight," said Sven. "We have heard of some Reds near here, and we are going to try to spot them."

Of course Vaino was not tired.

While they changed into white skiing cos-
tumes which would hide them against the
snow, Sven went on, "This is unofficial, and
I don't expect any danger, or I wouldn't take
you. But if I say RUN, you run, do you understand? I'm your colonel."

Vaino felt ready to obey anything.

They were moving silently through the
woods, about fifteen minutes run from the
camp, when three figures suddenly appeared
ahead of them.

"Who goes there?" called Sven, and Vaino
heard the click of his pistol cocking.

"Runeberg."

Great relief. The name of the Finnish
poet was the White password just then. The
three dim figures joined them, and they
glided silently on in a world washed into
varying shades of gray, and punctuated by
dark masses of mysterious trees.

After a while they heard a sound of voices.
They stopped, and Vladimir went on alone.
Soon he came back. "Delicious," he said, and

the six of them whispered together. Then they all crept forward.

They came to the wooded top of a hill, and looked down onto a little lake. The low hills ringed it on three sides, and a narrow inlet formed a pass at the foot. On the level ice a party of Reds had built a fire. There were about twenty-five of them, Russians and Finns. They had stacked their arms, some were wrapped in blankets asleep, the others were sitting in a circle laughing and talking, and taking nips out of vodka bottles which they were passing around. Evidently they felt safely hidden, sheltered from the wind, and thoroughly comfortable.

"Sven, stay here with the boy," whispered Vladimir. "Blix and I will go around to the far side. The other two stop in the middle. Anyone who meets a sentry is to fire twice as a warning. Otherwise, when I shout and fire together, that's the signal."

The four men slid away. Sven took his pistol and handed it to Vaino. "When you hear

[118]

On the Level Ice a Party of Reds Had Built a Fire

the signal fire with this. Bang your stick on a tree with the other hand, and shout as loud as you can. I'll use my rifle. Aim down, reload and go on firing till I say stop. Try to see that we are not both reloading at the same time. If you see them start up this way, run like the dickens." He paused and looked at Vaino remorsefully. "I shouldn't have brought you."

"Oh, I can make my voice sound like a man's when I shout. You'll see I can," answered Vaino, and clenched his teeth to keep them from chattering.

They waited. The laughter of the Reds came up to them, but no sound from the other side. The trees creaked occasionally with the frost. It was cold.

At last! A shot and a shout from across the lake. Vaino and Sven began firing. Vaino banged the tree with his free hand, and roared as low and as loud as he could. The noises came from every direction, crackled to and fro, echoing in the frosty air. It was bedlam.

[119]

The bewildered Reds picked themselves up, turned wildly around, then as shots splintered the ice from every side, one of them broke away and ran for the inlet. The others followed like panic-stricken sheep.

"Come on, men!" shouted Sven, banging his skis on the snow, and still shooting. "Hurrah for class consciousness! Hurrah for class consciousness!!"

"Save your bullets! Chase them with knives!" yelled a fierce voice from the middle.

As the last Red disappeared through the inlet, Vladimir shot out of the woods and down the slope, swearing at the top of his lungs in Russian. Now the others darted down, making straight for the stacked arms. Still shouting they fell upon them, and each one slung as many as he could carry around his shoulders, firing an occasional shot for good measure in the direction of the inlet. They loaded themselves with cartridge belts, they stuffed hand grenades in their pockets.

The first one with a full load started back up the hill.

"Go with him, and wait at the top," said Sven to Vaino.

He and Vladimir were throwing the four or five rifles that no one could manage into the fire. Then they too climbed the hill with a sound of cartridges popping merrily behind them.

"That will keep them away for a minute," said Sven, somewhat breathlessly. "Come Vaino. Let's get out of here in case they sneak back."

Vladimir, who was laughing so that he had collapsed against a tree, shook his head, but he started off with the others. The triumphal procession returned silently except when one of the overloaded conquerors stumbled, and his spoils clanked together, but they were not received silently at the barracks when they piled their trophies in the middle of the room.

When the congratulations were over,

Vaino flung himself on the floor with the rest of the soldiers, and slept without dreaming.

It was still dark when he was awakened by Sven shaking him.

"Get up, little brother. We've had word that the Reds may attack any minute. You must make tracks for home."

Sven wouldn't even let him stop for breakfast, but brought him a cup of hot coffee, and gave him some bread and some chocolate to chew as he went. Stiff and hungry as he was, when he stumbled out into the knife-sharp gray air, he felt himself very much a man for the part he had played in a man's adventure.

The journey back was as uneventful as it had been in coming, but it seemed endless to tired legs. When he had gone about three kilos he thought he heard distant shooting behind him, but he couldn't be sure. The noon sun was high when at last he reached home.

His mother must have been looking out

of the window, for she ran out to meet him in the courtyard and grabbed him tightly in her arms.

What a talk they had that afternoon! She was delighted with his news, and his adventures, but when he told her of the expected attack, and of thinking that he had heard shooting, she clasped her hands together and beat them up and down in her lap.

All that afternoon she was so restless, so unlike herself that Vaino didn't know what to make of it. After lunch he curled up on the sofa and went to sleep. When he woke up it was dark, and his mother was still in the courtyard with a shawl over her head, looking up the road to see if she could catch anyone coming by with news.

Vaino went and persuaded her to come in out of the cold, but when he got her inside he didn't know how to keep her away from the window. At last he went and stood behind her.

"Do come and sit down and tell me a story, Mother. Do please."

"Little son, how can I remember one?"
she answered still looking out.

"Tell me the one about Ahti's mother, and
what she did for her son when he went to
fight."

Fru Lundborg turned, and putting her
hand on his head, smiled down at him.

"Thank heaven I have you, Vaino. You
are a clever child."

She went back to the stove and picked up
her knitting.

Death's River

Word of the enchanting Maid of Pohja
came not only to Vaino and Ilmarinen. It
came also to Ahti, Ahti the merry, who leapt
higher in the dance than all the lads of the
village, who whirled the maidens until their
unbound hair flew out straight behind them,
and kissed them on their rosy cheeks when he
had finished, Ahti the mischievous, the boy
who would not grow up.

Although he had a wife so beautiful that the sun and the moon had sought her for their children, Ahti was angry with her because she had broken a promise to him, so he put her away to seek the Maid of Pohja.

"Dear son," cried his mother, "why run off to battle in strange lands when I have brewed the finest beer in this very house, and you may drink and sing all day if you will only stay at home?"

"What is home brewed beer to me, when I shall taste the mead of battle?" said Ahti, slapping his chest. "Bring my war shirt black with serpent's blood. Single-handed I shall overcome the people of Pohja, and take from them their gold and their silver."

"How odd you should mention gold," exclaimed his mother, for it just happens that this morning our slave ploughed up a chest full, so we have all the gold we need under this very roof."

"What is the good of gold not won in

battle? There may be a girl in Pohja who would like a kiss from the best of men."

His mother brought the shirt with trembling hands, but as he put it on she went on arguing.

"Oh my dear son, don't go to Pohja! You are not old enough, you have not magic enough to meet such mighty wizards!"

"You seem to forget, Mother, that I am no longer a child. Didn't I overcome three shamen from Lapland only last summer? Naked they stood on a rock all night, trying to sing me into the mud. Now they dwell in Tuonela, and *I* sent them there!"

He went on with his preparations, brushing his glossy hair, and admiring his handsome face in the mirror until his mother was nearly frantic.

"I don't care how much magic you have, dear boy. How can you sing against those people, when you don't even know their language?"

Then Ahti flew into a rage. He hurled his

comb of bone against the wall, and shouted,
"When that comb bleeds, you will know that
I am dead." With that he flung out of the
house, not forgetting, however, to snatch up
his sword as he went, for even the bravest
warrior feels stronger with a weapon.

He ran down to the meadow at the edge
of the woods, mounted on a high blue rock,
stretched out his arms, and shouted,

"Warriors of old, arise,
From the earth and from the Rivers!
Woodland, send me all thy dwarfs,
Forest arrows in their quivers!
Water maidens, robed in green,
Give my enemies the shivers!
If this should not be enough,
I have other help in store.
Ukko, highest over all,
Thou who taught the clouds to roar,
Save me with thy holy fire
From the spells my foes implore!"

Then he whistled up his golden maned
horse, sprang at one leap from the rock to its

back, harnessed it to a sledge, and drove off at a tremendous speed.

The silver sand flew like spray from his runners as he whirled down the beach, the heather crackled beneath him as he raced through the meadows. One, two, three days Ahti drove, and on the third he came to the grim gray village of Pohja.

At the first house he reined back and peered in the window. "Hola! Is no one here to hold my horse?"

There was only a child playing on the floor. "No one," said the child.

Ahti cracked his whip over his panting steed, and rattled on to the middle of the village.

"Hola! Is no one here to hold my horse?"

There was only an old woman nodding on a bench by the fire. "Plenty to take sticks to you!" she croaked.

"May they beat you first!" cried Ahti, gaily, and thundered on through the town. At the far end was the hall of the mistress of Pohja. As he neared it, Ahti called on the powers of Hiisi, the home of black magic, to stop the mouths of the dogs. That is why they did not bark when he drove into the courtyard.

He smote his whip on the ground, and a cloud of dust rose up. When it had cleared away, there stood a dwarf, who seized his horse, and rapidly unhitched it. Ahti strode up to the house, and a strange singing came out to him.

He dug away a little of the moss between the logs, and put his eye to the chink. The hall was full of shamen, magicians, wizards and seers. They sat on the benches around the board, squatted by the fire and even perched on the rafters, singing their slow rolling songs of magic. By the hearth crouched the best bard of Pohja making a song of Hiisi.

Ahti disguised himself a little, and stalked in.

"Hola! The shortest verses are the best.

It is better to keep quiet than to sing and be
interrupted!"

"We used to have dogs," said the mistress
of Pohja. "Who are you that you can push
past them?"

"Ho!" answered Ahti, "I've not come
here without even enough magic to stop a
dog barking? On three moonless summer
nights, on nine moonless nights of autumn,
my mother washed me, singing magic in
strange tongues. Should you like to hear it?"

Before anyone could answer, Ahti began to
sing, bounding lightly in a circle, and stamping out the cadences. He flung open his fur
coat, fire flashed from his eyes, he waved his
arms and shouted magic words. The best of
Lapland's singers were stricken dumb, their
sorcerers, their swordsmen, were sung into
stone, or lost in rushing rivers. Only one man,
Markahattu, the blind cowherd, escaped the
loud and cheerful songs of Ahti.

"You are too insignificant to bother
with!" Ahti shouted to him, making one last

bound in their air, and bringing his song to an end.

Black rage prevented Markahattu's answer, but he hurried out, tapping angrily with his stick as he went, and he did not stop until he had hidden himself beneath the waterfall of Tuonela, the dark land, the dread land. There he lay in wait for Ahti, for the time when he should journey homeward.

2

Ahti bent over with his hands on his knees, and grinned at Louhi. "Well, now, old woman, how about giving me your prettiest daughter?"

But Louhi still had a few tricks of her own. "My daughter must marry a man who can do more than sing. Now if you could only capture the Elk of Hiisi, from the far white fields——"

"I have a bow and a spear, all I need for that is a pair of snowshoes!" cried Ahti, and

[131]

he hurried off to find old Kauppi, the best snowshoe maker in Lapland.

"What is the use?" asked Kauppi. "The Elk is only a log of rotten wood when you get it."

"Never you mind that, wise old man. You just make the shoes!" shouted Ahti impatiently.

Kauppi made the shoes. He took a winter to one, and an autumn to the other. He lined them with otter fur, put rings on them of foxskin, and greased them with the fat of reindeer.

"Do you know how to run on these, young fellow?" he asked.

"Of course," cried Ahti, who had never tried them. He bound them on, took his bow and his spear, and ran off toward the fields of unbroken snow, singing as he ran.

"I am far the best of heroes,
    And this is true,
  There is nothing swift on four feet,
    That I on two,

Cannot overtake and capture,
On my snowshoe!"

Now Hiisi, king of malice, heard the laughing song of Ahti, and laughter is hateful to the black heart of Hiisi. He built an elk of rotten timber, with willow twigs for horns, water-lily flowers for eyes, and water-lily leaves for ears, bound by sinews of dried grass, and covered with a hide of pine bark.

"Go to Pohja, dear Thing," whispered Hiisi, "and make this Ahti sweat!"

The elk bounded into the air on its delicate feet and sprang off over the fields of unbroken snow until it came to Pohja. It rushed through the village, through the houses, upsetting the tubs, kicking the meat into the fire, knocking over the children. The dogs were barking, the children crying, the women screaming. Ahti heard the commotion and heard the elk bounding into the forest. He turned and ran in the direction of the noise. On and on he ran on his swift skis,

[133]

flying down the ridges like a swallow, pushing himself over the unbroken fields with his stick, while the snow flew like smoke from his path. Fast as he went the elk went faster. He heard its polished hooves crunch on the snow far ahead, but he could not see it. With the breath he had left he sang,

> "Help me hunt, Lappmen!
> Children, gather wood!
> Women, clean the pans!
> Elk will taste so good!"

From the top of a hill where the snow stretched down, Ahti saw the elk bounding below. Like an arrow from his bow he shot down the slope, with a white cloud of snow flying behind. Nearer and nearer to the elk he came. He made a last mighty leap, and caught it by a leg. The elk fell, quivering, in the snow. Ahti grasped its antlers and sat down beside it.

When he caught his breath he began to tickle it on its stomach. "That was easy!

Good old elk! Now if we had some girls here, we could have some fun!"

The elk trembled with rage, but lay quiet. Ahti grew confident and relaxed his hold. With one bound the elk tore itself free, and sprang off. Ahti, ruddier than ever, scrambled to his feet, and started after it, but, not looking where he was going, he stumbled into a hole and broke the point of first one ski and then the other. The elk, tossing its branched head, disappeared in the distance, and Ahti remained in the snow, looking ruefully at his broken skis.

For some time Ahti, far from merry, sat in the snow, wondering how he should reach home. At last he began to cheer himself up. "If I couldn't catch it, nobody could. Hereafter people had better let it alone." With that he had the happy idea of calling on the wood-nymphs, with their honey sweet flutes, and the king and queen of the forest, and Ukko himself, to help him.

[135]

Then power came back to the broken skis, and Ahti started out again. Two days and two nights he wandered in the far white fields, and on the third, clambering with great toil to the top of a mountain, he came suddenly upon the house of Tapio, the forest king.

In times of successful hunting the house of Tapio is a three-towered castle of stone, whose windows are framed in gold, and his household go in golden gowns, with golden bangles chiming upon their foreheads and their wrists.

Today the house was like the low-roofed hovel of a peasant, and the wood nymphs were clad in rags and birchbark shoes meet for the threshing. It boded ill for Ahti, that they did not wear the golden garments of good fortune, in which they give game to the lucky hunter, but Ahti was not dismayed. He stuck his head through the window, and shouted:

"Tapio, moss cloaked forest king,
　Robe the woods in beauty while I sing,
　As in happy days when trees drip honey,
　And the forest teems with elk and
　　bunny.

　Bid thy sweet maidens drive the game
　　toward me,
　And with my gold I will richly reward
　　thee,
　If it runs slowly, take a birch switch
　　to it,
　If it runs swiftly, jump thou the ditch
　　to it.
　If there are obstacles to break th'em
　　thou shalt go,
　Over the rivers silk bridges thou shalt
　　throw.
　Then thou shalt have my gold for thy
　　labors,
　Silver and copper untold for thy
　　labors."

For a week Ahti ran through the forest,
singing this song, and at last the maidens of
Tapio were so charmed that they surrounded

the elk and drove it toward the singer. Ahti
swung his rope, and again he caught it, and
this time bound it fast. Then he turned his
purse upside down, and as the gold and silver
poured out on the snow, he cried to Tapio,

"Spread your cloth,
  I keep troth.
  To catch gold that's glittering
  Can't be a bitter thing."

He left the gold on the snow, and bounding for joy, set off to Pohja, leading the elk.
  "Now, old woman," he cried to Louhi,
"here is the elk, where is the girl?"
  Louhi was ready for him. She pursed her
withered lips together and answered, "I
meant to mention it before. I should like to
marry my daughter to the man who could
bring me Hiisi's fiery colt, whose hooves are
steel and whose mane is a flame, out of Hiisi's
enchanted meadow."
  Ahti took off his snowshoes, picked up a
bridle and a bit, and without even stopping

to think of an appropriate song, turned eastward in search of the enchanted meadow. On the third day he reached it, and climbing on a rock peered through the farthest fence. There pranced the fiery colt with foam flecked mouth, and the sun behind it made an aureole of whirling flames about its head.

Ahti called it, but it galloped away from him. Although he was fleet of foot, he was no match for the colt, the fleetest thing under heaven. Fire flashed from its eyes, fire flew from its hooves. It sprang and swerved and pranced, and Ahti after it. At last he leaned against a fence, exhausted.

"Ukko!" he gasped. He had no breath for more.

Above him the clouds gathered softly. From the darkened heaven came blocks of hail, larger than a man's fist. Ahti took shelter under a tree, and the colt, bewildered, dodging the hail stones, ran in beside him. Then Ahti slipped the halter over its head, and forced the bit into its soft brown muzzle.

"Pretty colt, don't be sorry I have caught you. You shall be guided with silken cords, and you shall never be beaten."

With that he sprang on the back of the colt, and dashed off to Pohja. But when he again asked for the Rainbow, old Louhi smiled her toothless smile and said,

"I really meant to mention it before, but I wanted to be sure of other things first. I could only give my daughter to the man who could bring down the Swan of the river of Tuonela with one shot."

The river of the Tuonela is black and swift, and it rolls between the land of the living and the land of the dead. On its breast floats the Swan, the one white gleam in a world of blackness. To this dark and dangerous river Ahti came, merry and heedless as usual.

Beneath the falls Markahattu, the blind herdsman whom Ahti had despised and forgotten, lay waiting. All this while he had hidden in communion with the deadly things, with serpents, and poisonous plants, diseases and wolves, and every danger. He sent a serpent, and the serpent struck Ahti above the heart.

Ahti fell to his knees. "Alas," he cried, "I never learned the origin of serpents. I cannot harm them. I need only two words perhaps. I do not know them. Mother, I am too young to die! Life is so merry!"

Then Ahti fell forward with his face in the dark and rushing waters, and the waters closed over him. His body floated to the door of Tuonela and there was hacked in pieces and cast back into the stream, to float about forever, never resting, in the cataract of Death.

3

Every evening Ahti's mother sat by her fireside and thought of him. Every evening she watched the stars and hoped that they smiled upon him. Every morning she looked at his comb, which lay always where his dear hands had thrown it and remembered with pride his high spirits, and the waves in his glossy hair.

Then came a dark day when the comb streamed blood.

Ahti's mother wept, but she did not stop to dry her tears. They flowed unheeded down her wrinkled cheeks as she gathered her skirts in both hands, hurried out of the door, and started, half running, half walking, for Pohja. You might have thought that such an aged woman would fail on the long and perilous journey. Once or twice, it is true, she stopped and pressed her hands to her heart, but only for a moment. At the end she stalked past the dogs of Pohja without even seeing them, and confronted Louhi in her own hall.

"Where is my son?" she asked.

"How should I know?" answered Louhi. "I sent him home with a horse and sledge. Perhaps the wolves got him."

"Nonsense. Wolves could not hurt him.

Tell me what you have done with him, or I
will break into your copper mountain and
smash your Sampo."

Louhi retreated a step, for she saw that
Ahti's mother was armed with the power
that is stronger than magic.

"I tell you, I haven't seen him since I gave
him a boat to go home in."

"Tell no more lies or I'll kill you myself.
What have you done with my son?"

Then Louhi saw that she had a mother to
deal with.

"Indeed I don't know. He captured the
elk, and he captured the colt, and I sent him
to shoot the Swan of Tuonela before he
should have my daughter, and he has never
come back."

Ahti's mother wasted no more time with
Louhi. She shed no more tears, but her eyes
were black and bright as she ran into the
forest where Ahti had gone. You should have
seen that old woman! With the cunning of a
wolf she slipped through the swamps. If a

bush stood in her way her frail hands tore
it up as if she had been a giant. If a brook
crossed her path she leapt it as if she had
been a doe. Rest she never thought of, nor
did hunger trouble her.

When she came to a tall oak she bowed
before it. "God's oak," she said, "have you
seen my little Son, my golden apple and my
silver staff?"

"My own woe is enough for me," answered the oak, "for the day is coming when
men will fell me, and chop me up for burning."

When she came to a path she bowed before it, and said, "God's path, have you felt
the feet of my little son, my golden apple
and my silver staff?"

"My own woe is enough for me," answered the path, "for tramping feet and gal-
loping hooves are heavy on me all the day
long."

When the moon rose at night she bowed
before it. "God's moon, have you seen my

little son, my golden apple and my silver staff?"

"My own woe is enough for me," answered the moon. "I must watch alone all the frosty nights, and wane when my time is come."

When the dawn broke, she bowed to it, and cried, "God's sun, have you seen my little boy, my golden apple, and my silver staff?"

"That I have," said the friendly sun. "He lies in the river of Tuonela, and he has been hacked into little bits."

Two slow tears trickled from the eyes of Ahti's mother, but she did not stop to dry them. She ran to Ilmarinen the Smith.

"Make me a rake," she said. Ilmarinen made the rake. It was heavy, but Ahti's mother took it on her shoulder and rushed off to the river, which lay dark and turgid between lowering cliffs. Shapes of horror floated in the mist above it, greedy hands reached up from its depths, everywhere it was dark and forbidding. Few human creatures dared approach that river. Ahti's mother went straight to the brink.

The friendly sun looked down on the old woman, who, armed with the force beyond magic, dared pit her withered body against all the black powers of Tuonela. In sympathy he descended to a birch tree, and shone so fiercely that his shimmering heat lulled the race of evil, the folk of Tuonela, into slumber.

Ahti's mother did not notice the heat, scarcely gave him a grateful glance as he sailed back into the heavens. She had already waded into the dread black river, and was raking the bottom with her iron rake, searching for Ahti.

Farther and farther from shore she felt her way, until the black water swirled about her waist, and at last she fished up his hat. She held it to her breast for a moment, while the tears streamed from her eyes, then flung it on the shore, and went on with her raking.

The black water reached her armpits. It almost swept her off her feet, but she braced herself on her tottering legs and went on raking. The dark current whirled under her chin, it lapped treacherously against her lips, but she stood on tiptoe, and went on raking.

At last the rake stuck fast. With all her strength she pulled and hauled, and brought up from the water half of Ahti's body, and half his head. She carried this fragment to shore, and rested a minute, sitting down and cradling it in her arms.

"No use, no use," croaked a raven behind her.

"Of use to me," answered Ahti's mother. She laid the fragment lovingly on the shore, and waded back with her rake into the water.

Bit by bit she collected Ahti from the waves, and fitted him together, bone to bone, and joint to joint, caressing him with her knotted fingers. She called the goddess of the veins to give him fresh blood, and Jumala himself to knit him together, and so at last she made a whole man of him, but he could not speak.

She called on the bee to gather honey from the woods that she might anoint his mouth and the bee brought it to her, but it did no good. Then she spoke with sweet flattery to the bee, and begged it to bring honey from far away, but that, too, failed. At last she implored the bee to sail to the ninth heaven and bring her Jumala's own nectar.

"How can I ever fly so far?" asked the bee.

"Why that is nothing, dear little birdlet," she cried cajolingly. "Sweet little furry bee with gauzy wings, just let the wind lift you up to Orion's shoulders, and then it will be easy."

So she persuaded the bee to try, and in time he came back with the honey. Ahti's mother tasted it and was delighted to find that it was Jumala's own ointment with which he healed all the hurts in the world. Carefully she rubbed Ahti's body with it, calling on him tenderly the while. Then to her unutterable joy Ahti stretched himself and spoke. Eagerly she questioned him, eagerly she asked him how he had come there, and he told her of the herdsman, and how it had been a serpent that had undone him because he did not know the charm against it.

"There now," said his mother, "I told you, dear child, that you did not know enough to go against the Lapps. To think of trying it without even knowing the charms against serpents! It is a simple matter, for thus did they arise. From the spittle of Syojatar the witch, which cast upon the sea."

Then the mother looked fondly at her son, whom she had fashioned a second time with her feeble strength and her love and her prayers.

"Is there anything else you want, my darling?" she asked.

"Well," said Ahti, "I would just like to shoot that swan and get the girl."

But when he saw how pale his mother

grew, and how she trembled and how white
her hair became, he allowed himself to be
persuaded to go home with her. He helped
her to her feet, for she was only a weak old
woman who leaned on him feebly, and her
tired eyes rested always on his face.

"I could never have done it alone," she
said, and falling on her knees she gave thanks
to Jumala, the Creator.

* * *

When Fru Lundborg finished the story,
Vaino leaned his head against her knee.

"You would do all that for Sven or me,
wouldn't you, mother?"

"If I only could, son. All that and more.
All that and more."

She closed her eyes for a minute, and to
Vaino's horror two large tears squeezed
themselves out and ran slowly and silently
down her face. Before he could think of
what to do she had brushed them away, and
was looking at him like her old self.

All the rest of the week they had only fragments of bad news. Next morning an old peasant drove past and told them that there had been a fight near the barracks, and that the defeated Whites had fled in every direction. Some said they were going to reunite in Borgo. They did, but in a few days they were driven away from there, and from every other point where they tried to make a stand.

Fighting and running, fighting and running, and, in the end, pretty much all running. Their ammunition was failing. The Reds outnumbered them three to one. It was impossible to keep up with all the rumours. Fru Lundborg and Vaino would hear that the Whites were at a certain place, and before they could hitch up the pony to drive there, they would hear of another. They heard that the Reds took no prisoners. They heard that Sven had disappeared. They heard that he was wounded. They heard that he was safe. They heard that he was back with what was left of the corps. They couldn't tell what to believe, and what not to believe.

On the nineteenth of February they had a visit from Anniki. She came flying up the walk, her dark eyes shining, her face crimson, and shouted her news as she burst in the door.

"He's back, mother! He's here!"

"Sven?" cried Fru Lundborg, jumping up.

"Scarelius!"

Vaino longed to smack her.

His mother was wonderful. She showed no disappointment, but flung her arms around Anniki, and they cried together, and ended by laughing.

The Finnish brigade of the German army had landed in Vasa to join Mannerheim the day before, and Scarelius was with them! Anniki had heard the news from headquarters via the secret telephone to Mannerheim. Of course she could not talk to him, and she could get no letters, but just to know that he was on Finnish soil was enough for the present.

She had some news about the nearby White army also, but it was not very encouraging. They were scattered all over the countryside, in hiding. Some of their stores of ammunition had fallen into the hands of the enemy, and there was no longer any hope that they could make a stand against the Reds until help could reach them from Mannerheim, or perhaps from Germany. Their one chance was to escape in twos or threes over the ice, or to remain concealed until better times.

Several days dragged by, and still there was no word of Sven. They heard of occasional skirmishes here and there, but nothing of importance.

One morning, as Vaino was about to start out on his skis for the post-office in the neighboring village, to see if there were any letters he heard some firing in the direction of Sibbo. He unstrapped his skis and ran back in the house, to tell his mother. Old Marta threw her apron over her head, and began to moan until Fru Lundborg spoke sharply to her.

"Vaino, there is a box under the bed in Anniki's room, with four rifles and two pistols in it. Take the rifles out and bury them in the snow drift in the corner of the courtyard. We will keep the pistols, I don't expect to need them, but we had best have them in case we do. While we are at it we had better put the silver under the snow, too."

Any emergency threw Fru Lundborg into a fever of activity. It was her way of wringing her hands. For twenty minutes the three of them worked furiously, and by the time they had finished they heard no more shots. Vaino was hurrying with the silver when he saw a man, staggering like a drunkard, run through their gate.

"Mother! Mother!" screamed Vaino, "It's Sven!"

Sven was a sight. His cap was lost. He was

in his stocking feet. His boots were so much too big for him that he had taken them off in order to run faster, and was carrying them under his arm. His trousers were too big and the safety pin which fastened them had given way, so that he had to hold them up with his free hand. He had cut the insignia from his uniform in order to look as civilian as possible.

At first he was so out of breath that he could not speak but as soon as they got him in the house he told Vaino to hitch up the pony and drive down the road about a kilo to find Vladimir, who had been wounded in the leg, and who was hiding there.

Vaino was to sing a certain song as he went. Vladimir would show himself when he heard it, but Vaino must make sure that there was no one about before he started singing.

"I think we have thrown them off," said Sven, "for most of them went in the opposite direction, but just in case I am mistaken perhaps I had better get up in the attic, Mother, and I would like a bite to eat."

Vaino had already run out to hitch the pony to the sleigh. When he had driven about two kilos, and found the road perfectly empty on every side, he turned around and started back, singing at the top of his lungs. A man crawled out of a snow-covered thicket and lifted himself painfully to his feet. Vaino stopped.

"Hello, little enemy," said Vladimir, looking pale, but smiling. "You always bring luck. Give the old man a hand into the barouche."

Vaino jumped down and steadied him as he climbed stiffly in. One trouser leg was red and wet from the knee down. The way Vaino had sung before was nothing to the way he sang now, driving home with Vladimir hidden under the rugs in the sleigh.

Fru Lundborg and Marta came out and helped to carry him in. Vaino took the horse to the stable, and cleaned one or two blood

stains off the sleigh with snow. By the time
he got back to the house Vladimir was sitting
upstairs by a great fire in Sven's room, with
his leg neatly bandaged in clean linen,
stretched out on a pillow. Sven was smoking
on the other side of the fire. Fru Lundborg
thought that the attic would be too cold for
them, and that they would have time to get
up if anyone came, but that they should
sleep there at night, in case of surprises. She
and Marta were down in the kitchen, cooking the most splendid meal that she could
think of.

"It was just a flesh wound," said Vladimir.
"It'll be as good as ever inside a week."

"That looks like our last stand," said Sven.
"It's a great war when you have no guns."

February was almost over. In a couple of
weeks, with any luck, the ice would start to
break up in the bay, and then they could get
over to Reval, in Esthonia. The German
peace with Russia had not lasted. They were
fighting again, and Reval had fallen to the

Germans only a day or two before. There
was nothing for Sven and Vladimir to do but
to hide there at home until the crossing was
possible.

5

The Friendly Ice

FOR a short interlude of two weeks they were all very happy. Vaino never tired of hearing Vladimir and Sven tell about their experiences, and of looking with awe at the bullet hole in Sven's overcoat, right through the sleeve, and the healing scar on Vladimir's leg. Fru Lundborg was busy from morning till night, cooking for them, joking with them.

The two men made a great pretense in the beginning of having forgotten how to eat with knives and forks. Vladimir asked if it would not be more refined for him to drink his beer with a spoon. It took all of five days to persuade him to join Sven for an old fashioned Finnish bath in the steamy bath house, ending with a roll in the snow. He developed quite an appetite at last and almost had color in his thin cheeks.

"Will we never be rid of the greedy Russians?" Fru Lundborg would say with an exaggerated sigh, as she took an empty plate away from him, but if he did not eat what she thought he should she scolded him as if he had been one of her own sons.

The fear that the house might be searched by the Reds added only a pleasant dash of excitement to the peace of their days, but there was one shadow which they could not throw off. What was the matter with Mannerheim, up there in the Northwest? He did not move forward. He took no towns, won no victories. The Reds were growing stronger and stronger, preparing for a great offensive on the tenth of March, and nothing was done to prevent it. Resistance in the South was crushed. The Northwest was the only hope.

"Does he exist, this Mannerheim?" asked Vladimir, who was not a patient man.

Then one evening after dark, Anniki came out to the house, very quietly, on foot.

"Mother," she said, I'm to take the night train for Tammerfors at the station beyond the city. Will you drive me there? The secret telephone to Mannerheim has been discovered and cut at Bjorneborg by the Reds, and I am to go up with a message.

She tried to speak calmly as she hurriedly made a little package of some things but there were bubbles of joy all through her voice.

Vaino went out to hitch the pony to the sleigh. When he came back Anniki was dressed in Marta's Sunday best, looking very fat around the waist, like a peasant woman on a holiday. Sven and Vladimir were excitedly wishing her luck. She kissed them all around, and then she and Fru Lundborg got into the sleigh and drove off together.

Sven grumbled about not being able to take her himself, but it was too dangerous for him on the roads. He let Vaino sit up with him until their mother came home. When she got back her eyes were red, and she said very little, except for one general remark about being proud of her children.

After that the days slipped by as before. Vladimir and Sven played patience, read all the books in the house, and the "Family Journal" from cover to cover, and sent Vaino out twice a day to get information about the ice. They had told all their stories by now, and Fru Lundborg was again called upon for hers in the evenings as they sat around the stove.

Several days after Anniki had left, a strange man knocked at the door, handed a letter without an address to Fru Lundborg, and hurried away into the darkness. When she had glanced through it she called the family together, and read it aloud to them.

"Darling Mother and Brothers:

"This is my first chance to send a letter telling you not to worry.

"I got here so easily that you would hardly believe it. Nobody questioned me on the train. At Tammerfors I went to a certain house, changed, picked up a companion, and we started off on skis like two girls on a holiday. We saw one or two Red sentries before they saw us, and we met one, but we looked so innocent, and spoke such good Finnish, that he let us through. By four o'clock we had found Mannerheim, but I may not say where, nor what he is doing.

"I have some news of my own, however. Scarelius is here, and he and I were married last night by the Lutheran priest who is with them. We will have the banns properly when we get home, but this is wartime.

"I am sorry darling Mother, to cheat you out of the wedding that we have talked about since I was a little girl, but I know you understand, and love us both.

"I shall stay on here for some work. May the day soon come when we all return in triumph! Meanwhile, don't worry, I am safe, and happier than I have ever been. I send you all a thousand kisses.

VOIMA."

"I think she has a terrible nerve to go off that way and get married without letting mother know. Just thinking of herself all the time. She's selfish, that's what she is," exclaimed Vaino.

"Wait until you are in love before you judge her," answered his mother, smiling.

"I'm never going to fall in love. It makes people so silly. Sven's not in love."

"It might creep up on him any day," said Vladimir. "They say it sometimes begins with a rash on the ears. Do you see any signs of it?"

Vaino was relieved to find that there were none.

When they asked Fru Lundborg for a story

that evening, she protested that she could think of nothing but weddings, but she would tell them about a wedding which had really come off in the proper style, and so she began.

———

The Capture of the Rainbow

Ahti perished, and was saved by the love of his mother, but the Rainbow still dwelt unwed in the far Northland, and those who had seen her could not forget her. Hers was a beauty like the whirling streamers of light which break the night of winter over icy fields. Now she had been wooed by Vaino, the wisest, Ilmarinen, the strongest and most skillful, and Ahti, the merriest of men, and all of them had gone away in sorrow. But Vaino did not forget.

Vaino built himself a boat. He did not use the hollow aspen, nor the knotted pine, but the sturdy oak for the keel and the prow. He built it with care, and many magic songs went into the building, but when he had done

what he could, the boat was still unfinished.
Three words were needed to make it right.
All of his spells were unavailing. The three
words he did not know.

Vaino searched in the brains of swans and
swallows, beneath the tongues of squirrel and
reindeer. The three words were not there.

"In dark Tuonela," said Vaino, "all secrets
are known. There I shall search for the three
lost words."

Vaino was old and unafraid. He stalked
through the swamps and the thickets, he
came to the brim of Tuonela's dread river,
and he shouted for a boat. The dwarf girl of
Tuonela, who rows the dead to their last
dim home, heard his shouting.

"Why do you come here?" she asked,
"Disease or death have not overtaken you."

"Death himself brought me," answered
Vaino.

"That is a lie," said the dwarf girl. "Tuoni walks with those he brings. Why are you
come?"

"Steel sent me, water drowned me, fire burnt me."

"Lies again," answered the girl. "Steel sends them bleeding, water dripping, fire scorching. Why are you come?"

Vaino laughed. "Perhaps I did lie a little, but there is no deceiving you. I built a boat, and to finish it, I need Tuoni's gimlet."

"Many come here, and all unwillingly," said the dwarf. "None return. Therefore go back while there is time."

"Do not seek to frighten me as if I were an old woman. Bring your boat."

In silence the dwarf girl did as he asked. In silence they started down the river. High black cliffs rose on either side, and darkened the black rushing water. Only a narrow strip of threatening sky showed above them. All was darkness. Ahead of the boat floated Tuoni's swan, silently leading the way. The dwarf girl wailed for Vaino, and the cliffs gave back her woe. Thus did Vaino come to Tuonela, in search of three lost words.

[167]

When he had passed through the outer court, where the guilty lie on red-hot stones, under a coverlet of writhing snakes, he refused food and drink, for the ale of Tuonela is death to the living, but he asked the mistress of the dead about the three lost words.

"There are no words here, but you are here, Vaino, and here you shall stay forever. Never while the golden moon is shining, while the silver sun is warm, shall you lay eyes upon your homeland."

Then indeed dread came to Vaino, and he laid him down on a bench, pretending to be asleep, but thinking how he might escape. While he lay, the witch of Tuonela, her sharp chin resting on her crooked knee, sat beside him, humming, and the three fingered wizard of Tuonela came and bore her company. In one summer night, in the short hour between darkness and dawning, she wove a thousand nets of copper, he a thousand nets of iron. As dawn broke, the witch and the wizard drew their thin gray rags about them,

[168]

and fluttered out to lay their nets across the dark river.

Vaino slipped from his bed and took on the form of a snake. When day was high, the wizard, using his three iron fingers like hooks, drew up the nets. In them were many strange fish, but not Vaino. In the form of a snake he had slipped through the meshes and already he was back in Suomi, singing joyfully of his escape.

Vaino looked at his unfinished boat, and reflected that as yet he had not found the three lost words. There was one who knew all the words of magic in the world, and over it and under it. That was Vipunen, the giant.

Before men came there was Vipunen. But when men peopled the earth, and when he had come to the fullness of all wisdom, he laid him down and slept, for he had nothing more to learn. Now a forest grew in his beard, and willows from his eyebrows. The path to him was made of needles. swords, and sharpest axes.

[169]

That did not trouble Vaino. He had Ilmarinen make him iron shoes, iron gauntlets, and an iron staff with a core of steel.

"You won't get even half a word from Vipunen," said Ilmarinen. "He's dead!"

Vaino set out. In his iron shoes, leaning on his iron staff, with his white beard and his blue cloak streaming behind him, he stepped swiftly over the sharp-edged path. Few could stride like Vaino. Soon he came to the place where Vipunen was sleeping like a mountain range, with a forest in his beard.

Vaino felled the forest with his sword. He thrust his staff into the giant's mouth, and the giant, goaded by the steel, closed his mighty jaws on it, but could not bite it through. As he opened them again, Vaino, standing on his lip, slipped and fell into the yawning cavern! Then Vipunen sang:

"I've eaten goats and pigs,
   I've feasted on a cow,
But the best I ever tasted,
   I taste right now."

Vaino had need of his wits. Inside Vipunen it was dark and hot, and his closed mouth was the only door. Vaino did not like it. But he was a man who could make much with a few tools, and although his hands were empty he had a knife with a wooden handle in his belt.

First he carved himself a boat from the handle, and sailed up and down inside Vipunen. But this did not disturb the giant. Then Vaino took the blade of the knife. With his knee for an anvil and his elbow for a hammer he began to pound away. Tap-tap-tap. Day and night he hammered and pounded inside Vipunen.

"Oh! Oh!" cried the giant, "What is in me now? Sparks come up in my throat, and fire burns in my belly. Get out, Thing, before I tell your mother!"

Vaino hammered until he was out of breath.

"Are you a disease from the good Lord Jumala? Or from the powers of evil? Or

were you bribed to come? If you came from
the quicksands, or the swamps, or the rotten
trees, or the den of a bear, or a battle field, or
the ooze of ocean, get you back to the place
of your beginning!"

Vaino had come from none of these places,
so he hammered harder than ever. Vipunen
called on the Earth Queen, the Water Queen,
the forest people, the Mother of all Living,
Ukko himself. When he paused for breath,
Vaino spoke.

"I'm perfectly comfortable here, of
course, but I might consent to go if you
would teach me all of your spells."

Vipunen would have done anything to
stop the hammering in his stomach. He began to sing. He sang the origin of the earth
and the sea and the sky, and all that is in
them. Creation stood still to listen to Vipunen. The sun rested in the tree tops, the
rivers halted in their rush to the sea, the
waves of the sea stood still.

When he had finished, "Open your mouth," said Vaino, "I shall go now."

Vipunen gaped wide, with his mouth like the mouth of a cavern. "It was good of you to come," he gasped, "but it is better when you go."

Vaino strode home. On his way he passed Ilmarinen.

"You didn't get much out of that dead giant, did you?" asked Ilmarinen, showing his firm white teeth.

"Only every spell in the world," answered Vaino.

He went home and finished his boat.

2

In the white film of morning, Vaino set out to sea in his boat. It was pale gray like the mist it traveled. Vaino hoisted a red sail on one mast, and a blue sail on the other. The winds blew at his command, and the water was smooth before him.

At a point on the shore where the black

bow of the pine woods curved behind, a red landing pier ran out into the water. On the pier stood Anniki, sister of Ilmarinen, called Daughter of Twilight, because of her dusky hair. She was washing her clothes by dipping them up and down in the clear still water.

In the distance she saw a speck on the sea, —neither a bird, nor a fish, nor an island. The speck grew nearer, and she hailed Vaino.

"Where are you going?" she called.

"Salmon fishing, in the deep and reedy river of Tuoni," answered Vaino.

"Don't try to tell me that," she shouted, cheerfully, "I know where salmon spawn."

Vaino said that he was hunting geese, but she could see that he had no dogs nor bows. He said that he was going to war, but she knew how men went to war. He asked her to come into his boat, but that made Anniki very angry. She screamed at him, jumping up and down until her long earrings jangled.

"Don't lie to me any more, Vaino!"

Vaino smiled into his beard. "I may have

lied a little. If you must know I am off to seek a maid in Pohja, where no grass grows, and no men plow, and the heroes eat each other."

Anniki stared at him with her little red mouth like an O. Then she dropped the wet clothes she was holding, caught her blue skirts in both hands, and ran like a squirrel to Ilmarinen, with her tin earrings flying about her head.

Ilmarinen stood over his forge, making an iron bench with silver mountings. For a minute Anniki was too out of breath to speak. She leaned against the door post, and shook both hands at him.

"What will you give me for what I know?" she cried at last.

Ilmarinen shook his soot-blackened hair out of his eyes, and smiled at his sister, while the red light shone on his sweat-gleaming body.

"Rings and a headdress for good news. Nothing for bad."

"Do you still want to marry that girl in Pohja?"

"Yes," said Ilmarinen, frowning.

"Well, while you stand there and hammer, winter and summer, somebody else is going to get her. Vaino has just gone past here in a boat!"

Ilmarinen was troubled. He flung his hammer on the ground, and the tongs slipped from his fingers.

"Do something about it!" cried Anniki.

"I will," shouted Ilmarinen, suddenly. "Heat the bath house. I must get rid of this winter's soot."

Anniki bounded off like a rabbit. She gathered sticks for a fire, heated stones and carried water, broke bath whisks from the bushes, got ashes to clean his body, and marrow fat soap for his hair. While she worked Ilmarinen forged the trinkets he had promised her, and poured them into her hands as he strode into the bath house.

What a bath Ilmarinen had!

When he came out, after steaming and switching and scrubbing, his hair was curling gold, his rosy cheeks shone like the moon, even his neck was as white as an egg. There wasn't a fleck of soot or a drop of sweat on Ilmarinen. Anniki clapped her hands in admiration, and cried, "I wouldn't have known you!"

She ran for a linen shirt, new trousers, fine blue jacket, a woolen coat, and a fur overcoat to go on top. She rummaged out a gold embroidered belt which his mother had made as a girl, and gold embroidered gloves. To crown it all she found a high-topped hat, the very hat that their father had worn as a bridegroom, and with her own hands she set it on his curls! Then she stepped back, round-eyed, and admired him.

Ilmarinen ordered his servant, for he kept a servant, and paid him in money, to bring up the best horse, and the best sledge, and six blue cuckoos to sit on the reins and sing. He waved a hand to Anniki, leapt in, and thundered off. He prayed to Ukko for snow to smooth the way, and the snow came!

For three days Ilmarinen guided his whitebrowed horse along the shore, until at last he came abreast of Vaino, sailing quietly not far out to sea. He drove out until the water came to the edge of his sleigh, and standing up he shouted with all the strength of his mighty lungs.

Vaino heard him, and turned his boat shoreward.

"Vaino," cried Ilmarinen, in a voice like summer thunder, "let's make a bargain not to take the girl by force, but to let her choose between us!"

Vaino had to agree in view of all Ilmarinen had done for him. So they travelled, one on the sea, one on the shore, and came to Pohja together. The watch dog barked.

"Go see what is the matter," said the master of Pohja to his daughter.

"I haven't time, I have the corn to grind."

"You go, Louhi."

"You talk too much. I have dinner to get."

"Women are always busy lying around in front of the fire," grumbled the master of Pohja. "I'll go myself."

He came back and told Louhi what he had seen. Louhi bade her waiting maid lay the best log on the fire over faggots of holy rowan.

"If it drips water they are friends, if blood foes, if honey, suitors," she said.

In a few moments the log dripped honey.

"My Daughter of the Rainbow," said Louhi, "two men are hurrying to Pohja. In a gray boat, with sails of blue and crimson, comes Vaino. He has all the wisdom in the world, his boat is filled with treasure, he is old and kind. No man is so rich or so wise as Vaino. In a sledge of many colors sits Ilmarinen, empty handed, and six blue cuckoos sing on his reins. When they come, fill a tankard, and give it to your choice.

Vaino arrived first, and hurried in, singing:

[179]

"Maid of Rainbow beauty, long desired,
Come and nestle dovelike in my arms,
I have built earth's noblest boat, inspired
Solely by the longing for your charms."

"I don't like sailors," said the Rainbow,
"for the wind drives their thoughts seaward,
and the east wind makes them sad."

Just then Ilmarinen drove up in his sleigh.
He ran into the hall, but as he reached the
door his feet dragged uncontrollably, his blue
eyes frowned, and he looked in embarrass-
ment from one to another. The maid of Pohja glanced shyly at his broad chest and strong
arms.

"I'll take the young one," she said, and
handed Ilmarinen the tankard.

Ilmarinen did not take it, for his eyes were
on the maiden.

"I shan't drink," he murmured, "until I
claim my bride."

Louhi was not pleased. She shoved herself
in between Ilmarinen and her daughter, and

when she smiled at him her smile was more terrible than a man's anger.

"This is all very well," she said, "but there will be one or two little things to do first. My son left half of the field of vipers unplowed the other day———"

This was too much like a former occasion. Ilmarinen twisted his high crowned hat in his hands. But he had an ally now in the maid of Pohja. She slipped from the room, and signed him to follow her. When he did, she advised him to make a golden plow and shoes of steel. With them Ilmarinen plowed the field without noticing the snakes as they hissed about his ankles.

But Louhi was exacting. She wanted the bear and the wolf of Tuonela.

"Forge bits and muzzles of iron while you sit on a rock in the middle of a waterfall," advised the maid of Pojha, when Ilmarinen found her, weaving, and singing as she threw the shuttle. Ilmarinen obeyed her, and brought back the bear and the wolf.

Still Louhi was not satisfied. She asked for a pike from the river of Tuonela, and she asked to have him caught without the use of nets or tackle. Ilmarinen did not know what to do about that.

"You can still use a bird to catch a fish," said the maid of Pohja, running her fingers through his golden curls. "Forge yourself an eagle."

Ilmarinen made the eagle, and mounted on its back. Its copper breast flamed like fire in the sun, it soared over the forests and over the sea, a wing swept the sky and a wing swept the water, and it came to rest on the cliffs by the river of Tuonela.

First they were attacked by a water kelpie. The eagle held him under the mud until he smothered. Then came the pike. His back was as long as seven boats, his teeth were like the teeth of a rake, and he opened his mouth to swallow Ilmarinen. The eagle struck at him.

Back and forth, into the water, and into

the sky they raged. At last the eagle sank his claws into the pike, and carried him away. In vain Ilmarinen, exulting on his creature's back, ordered him to bare the pike to Pohja. The eagle was hungry and the fire of battle flamed in his eye. He devoured the pike all but the head, and deaf to his master's reproaches, sailed into the sky. The clouds were cleft asunder by the beat of his iron wings, he broke the rainbow with his talons, soaring up and up, until the fire that flamed from his back was lost in the golden shining of the moon.

Ilmarinen took the head of the pike, and returning to Pohja, threw it down in front of Louhi as she sat by the door of the hall, rubbing her knotted hands over the head of her stick.

"Make a chair out of that. Now I shall take my bride."

Louhi was embarrassed, for she could think of nothing more to give him to do. She sucked her lips in and out, and stared at the toothy jaws which gaped like a cavern.

"You should not have feasted on the body of the prize," she said.

"It is hard to get anything undamaged out of Tuonela's river," answered Ilmarinen, standing his ground.

At last Louhi gave in, and she shuffled away to prepare for the wedding.

A hawk flew out of the sky,
    A hawk of the south.
He perched on the heroes' roof,
    But the iron withstood his mouth.

He perched on the copper roof
    Of the matron's hall,
But his sharp beak could not pierce
    Through the copper wall.

The roof of the maiden's bower
    Was linen thin,
With a single stroke of his beak
    The hawk came in.

Of all the fluttering ducks
    He chose the best,

And bore her off in his claws,
　To a hidden nest.

"Alas, alas," cried Louhi, wringing her
hands in lamentation. "How often have I
told my darling not to sit by the window, not
to show herself with unbraided hair in the
fields. It is easier to hide a long tailed horse
in a stall than a beautiful girl from the gal-
lants of Suomi, the terrible men who shoe
their horses with steel."

The preparations for the wedding went
forward. They slaughtered an ox so huge
that his flesh gave one hundred barrels of
meat, they built a hall so huge that a dog
barking at one end could not be heard at another, they made mead of barley and honey,
and they sent messengers in eight directions
to bid the guests to the feast. But they sent
no invitation to troublesome Ahti, and Ahti
was angry when he saw the smoke of the fes-
tival.

"Welcome to my miserable pine hut!"

cried Louhi, as the guests entered the vast
hall of apple and birch. They feasted and
they feasted, and while they feasted Vaino
sang, having first politely invited everyone
else to try, which all were wise enough to re-
fuse to do. Vaino sang in praise of every-
body, and never ran out of words.

The bridegroom stood like an oak in the
forest, the bride like a moon among stars.
They baited the bride, telling her how she
must leave her dear father and mother forever, and go to be a slave to her mother-in-
law, and so they brought her to tears, that
they might comfort her. They sang all the
old songs of weddings and feastings.

Wait, wait,
The flood is in spate,
But the bride is late
To greet her mate.
She must braid her hair,
Make her garments fair,
Lose her cheerful air,
Before she comes there.

[186]

AND WHILE THEY FEASTED VAINO SANG

"I have always longed for this hour, but I don't like it at all, I don't like it at all," sobbed the bride, but nobody paid any attention to her. They danced around her, and shook their fingers at her, and instructed her how she should comport herself in her new home, how she should do all the work of the household, and always answer sweetly to her mother- and father-in-law, and never complain that they treated her harshly. They told her that she must leave three things behind her, sleep in the daytime, her mother's love, and the best of food.

The bridegroom, too, came in for a share of advice. They cautioned him to be kind to her, and let her come home for visits, not to lock her out of the store-house where the good food is kept, to stand up for her against his family, and not to beat her.

Then the bride, weeping, sang her farewells. Farewell to her dear childhood home, to her father and her mother and her dog and her horse, and the cattle who lowed for her coming. Ilmarinen grew tired of the whole affair, picked her up in his arms, and shouldering his way through the shouting crowd, bore her out to the sleigh. Everyone waved, and the bride waved back.

"Don't forget to say farewell to the dear old tree stumps and mud holes," said Ilmarinen rather crossly. Then guiding his horse with one hand, he embraced his bride with the other, and drove off to the welcome prepared for her in his own home.

Vaino went back alone in his boat, and his head was bent in sorrow as he sang:

"Youth is the time to marry;
  In age love will only harry;
  If old contend with young men,
  They'll find themselves undone men."

* * *

The very next morning things began to happen. In the first place, when Vaino went down to the village for the mail, he heard two stone masons talking, and stone masons and Reds were the same thing.

"I tell you," said one of them, "the widow Lundborg is buying in too much food these days, and I saw a man walking in her courtyard when I passed there the other night. I'm going to report it to the government."

"Now don't be in a hurry, for it's never any use to rush at things," said the other, like a true Finn. "I'm going to Helsingfors tomorrow, and I'll report it there."

They moved out of earshot, and Vaino did not dare to be caught following them, so he sped home with the news. He found Sven and Vladimir already excited, for they had just heard that the ice was breaking in the bay, and that a successful crossing to Reval had been made. When they had listened to Vaino they decided at once to go that night.

A stout-hearted fisherman had already agreed to let them have his boat, and had told them of two other Whites hiding in a deserted villa up the beach, who would join them. Vaino was dispatched with messages. They were all to meet at the foot of the

Lundborg land that afternoon about four o'clock.

Fru Lundborg dashed out in her sleigh for some extra food, and when she came back, collected every piece of light warm clothing in the house and gave it to Sven and Vladimir. What they couldn't wear they could put in the boat, she said.

What a meal she gave them, at about half past two! She got out the great table cover which she had embroidered as a girl, and all the best china and glassware. After a glass of schnapps they had smorgasbrod, slices of brown and white bread with delicious things such as smoked salmon, raw eel, or cheese, laid on them. Then they had a hot thick soup with an egg in it. That was followed by a good fat goose, stuffed with prunes, with brussels sprouts, and cold potatoes, boiled in their skins. They finished off on clabber with black bread crumbs and brown sugar sprinkled over it, and washed down the whole with the best Rhine wine that could be found in the cellar.

It was hard to get all those things during the war, but it could be done by a determined woman, who had been driving about the countryside all morning.

After dinner they began to get dressed. They must have things that were warm, without being heavy, for they had a long walk ahead of them over the ice. Vladimir had holes in his boots, so he put in several copies of "The Workman," to protect his feet from the sharp splinters. Fru Lundborg made them up a package of bread and meat, and filled their flasks with brandy.

At about four they went out of the house, and Fru Lundborg and Vaino with them, as far as the edge of the pine woods. It was foolish perhaps for them to show themselves in daylight, but they could not bear to wait any longer. Fru Lundborg and Vaino were to say good-bye in the woods, and let them cover the last stretch to the shore alone, in order to attract as little attention as possible. From the edge of the woods they could see the rowboat, sitting on the ice, and the other two men, already beside it.

Fru Lundborg had been very gay all day, and she smiled as she kissed Sven good-bye.

"Do I dare to say farewell to you this time?" asked Vladimir.

For answer she put her arms around him and kissed him too.

"Take care of each other," she said.

They started down the hill toward the ice, without looking back. Through the pine branches Fru Lundborg and Vaino saw them wind the ropes about their arms and start forward, dragging the boat.

A strong wind had blown the snow from the boughs and made them hiss about the two who stood among them watching. The dark day was fading almost imperceptibly into dusk. Heavy gray clouds rolled down to meet the distant stretches of the pale gray ice. The four black specks which were the men and the larger speck which was the boat, melted together, advanced into the meeting grayness, and vanished there. The mother and Vaino turned and walked slowly back to the house.

Out on the ice the four men tramped two kilometres and a half, dragging the boat, in the first half hour. The coast had faded into a dim line against the lowerng sky. The grayness darkened. There was nothing to be seen on any side, only the vast gray spaces. There was nothing to be heard except their heavy tramp, and the scraping of the boat against the ice.

The gray deepened imperceptibly into black, and the black was one great emptiness. The weight of the boat grew heavier with every footstep, the wind grew sharper, and still they had not come to the open channel. They saw nothing but the endless stretches of the gray and empty ice. Here and there the ice had piled itself up into walls a meter high, and the heavy boat must be lifted over with a "one-two-three- hopp-hi!"

In the darkness they could no longer see the compass. The wind snuffed out their matches before they were alight. There were no stars. For interminable hours they plodded on in black and empty space, guided only by the numbing blast against their right cheeks.

From time to time they rested, altered the ropes which were cutting their arms, gnawed at a little bread with meat fat for butter, rubbed freezing noses with snow, stamped aching feet. Then on again in the cold silence, broken by an occasional distant roar of shifting ice. Still the channel did not appear.

At last they saw a black line between the dark ice and the darker sky, a line which widened as they neared it. Open water! It put new life in their weary feet, and they pushed on more quickly. Soon they heard a sound more beautiful to them than music, the slapping of the little waves against the ice, and the ice smoothed out beneath their feet. Then it groaned ominously under them. They were near the edge. Together they gave the boat a running start, leapt into it, and with a crackling and a grating splashed into the water.

This was freedom! This was joy! This was peace of mind! Now they were safe. There was open water between them and the Reds.

It seemed no time at all that they were rowing, while they laughed together, and listened to the song of the waves, and the indescribable mutterings of the ice chunks which floated past, until the boat grated once more against the solid ice. They struck out with their oars until the ice resisted them, then Vladimir, the lightest, sprang out on it. It held. The others followed him, one by one, Sven last, and with a tremendous pull, they hauled the boat up too.

They had no way of quenching their thirst after this exercise, so one by one, lying on their stomachs, they shoved themselves to the edge of the ice, and lapped up some of the brackish water of the Bay. Then congratulating each other they started out again.

Vladimir struck up a song, and the others joined in a lusty chorus:

When the darkness lifts,
And the air is soft,
And the new green leaves are uncurled,
Like the unchecked wave
From the free fresh bay,
We storm out into the world.

"What's this?" cried Vladimir, checking
the song and stopping abruptly. The others
stared at him. "The wind!" One by one they
collected their dazed faculties, one by one
they realized that the wind, which had blown
sharply and constantly on their right cheeks,
was coming from their left.

Sven fumbled for his compass, and making a shelter under his coat while the others
crowded around him, looked at it. It was true.
The channel was behind them, and they were
walking north over the ice,—to Finland.
Somehow they had turned the boat in rowing, and came back to the same side.

There was nothing for it but to retrace
their steps. They tried to go on singing, but
had no heart for it. This time the ice gave

way before they expected, and Sven nearly missed the boat. They pulled him in over the edge, wet to the waist. When they had crossed they made sure by compass and by wind that they were really headed southward to Esthonia.

Again the weary tramping. Again the long hours of dragging forward. Twice they stopped, and flung themselves down on the ice two at a time, only to be hauled up by the others before they could fall asleep. The smooth ice near the channel was soon forgotten as they stumbled through heavy crusty snow, and over great boulders. Their eyes watered as they struggled with sleep, and the tears froze on their cheeks. The weight of the boat became enormous.

The slow deliberate northern dawn crept up. Inch by inch the sun rose, and the clouds retreated gently. Around them they saw only the dazzling ice, the fantastic shapes of the snowy boulders. There was no land before them, no land behind them.

"Do you see those moving specks on the horizon?" asked Sven. "They must be fishermen."

For a moment they took heart.

"I see them," answered Vladimir, "but they are in our tired eyes. Look behind you. They are there too."

On, and on. They had ceased to be men. They were mechanical toys, set in motion long ago, and then forgotten. The toys were tired, their joints creaked, but they must jig, jig, jig, until they fell apart. They were prisoners tied to a heavy weight which thumped along behind them.

"Why don't you let go the boat and just walk for a bit, Vladimir?" asked Sven. "We can manage."

"Shut up," answered Vladimir, without opening his eyes.

The mirage of the shore grew more and more persistent. Time after time they were deceived by it, and each disappointment was harder to bear than the last.

A black dot moved over the ice. One after another, they looked at it, looked away, looked back again. This one was real. It was a man, coming toward them. They hailed him in chorus. The man approached and stared at them with vacant eyes.

"How far is it to shore?"

"Maybe four, maybe five kilo," said the man.

"Where are you going?"

"Over the ice to the Reds in Finland. The Germans are behind me."

"You are crazy, man. The ice has broken. You can't get there without a boat."

But the man seemed not to hear them. His war-fagged mind had room for only one idea. He broke away while they were still talking, and staggered on across the ice.

The Finns shrugged their shoulders and pressed forward. An hour, two hours, and still there was no sight of land. Was it possible that they had lost their way, and were heading out into the open sea? The compass

[199]

assured them that they had still the right direction.

The sun was covered by clouds, and a snow storm broke over their heads. The wind lashed them with their own clothing. The snow cut their faces, and hung on their lashes. Now they could not see more than a few meters ahead of them, so there was no question of looking for the coast. Only keep tramping on and on. Keep pushing one weary foot in front of the other. Keep dragging the boat.

The snow ceased to fall. It was after twelve o'clock. They must rest a little and choke the fear that was beginning to creep up in them. Had they really missed their way, and would they never reach the coast? Would they wander here on the ice until their strength failed, until they lay down, and found it impossible to get up again.

"You are the tallest, Vladimir. Get up on the boat, and see if you see anything."

Sven and the other two Finns were nearly exhausted. Their noses and their eyes were

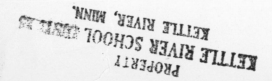

red and their stubborn faces were drawn together more stubbornly than ever. Vladimir
was as white as the ice. The smile with which
he had started was set on his face as if it had
frozen there. Only the thin wires of his
nerves held his body upright.

He climbed up on the boat, resting his
hand on Sven's shoulder, shaded his eyes and
stared into the gray distance. Then he
shouted:

"Land! Land!"

One after another they looked. They all
saw it. Three specks on the horizon. The
three little islands which lie off the coast of
Esthonia!

The boat seemed lighter as they took hold
of it again. For a little while they even had
breath to cheer each other with conversation.
But time went on, and the islands seemed
no nearer. The aches came back to the legs,
the heads drooped forward. The sun disappeared, and another slow dusk gathered.
They could not remember how many suns

they had seen on that walk, could not remember Finland.

But now there were specks on the ice which did not move when the head moved. They came nearer, and gave a friendly shout. They were Esthonian fishermen who needed no explanation from the travellers. These were not the first friends they had welcomed from across the ice. They looped the boat ropes over their own fresh shoulders, and under their guidance the shore, the incredible, legendary shore, loomed up at last in the darkness. They had been walking steadily for twenty-eight hours and had covered more than ninety kilometers.

It was a last interminable mile from the shore to the houses where they might find shelter. The three Finns plodded on, heads hunched into their shoulders, bent down into the wind, but Vladimir flung back his head like a runner crossing the tape, staggered like a drunken man, and refused all offers of help with acrimony.

At last a cottage door was flung open before them. They staggered over the threshold into light and heat. Vladimir was last. He leaned against the door post for a moment. Then when he thought he was not watched, lifted one leg in both hands and set it over the doorstep, reached back and helped the other to follow it. Inside he sank down the wall to the floor, his legs stretched out in front of him.

"I did it!" he said, looking up with a brilliant smile. Then his head dropped forward.

It was lovely and hot in the cottage. The windows had not been opened since the previous summer. There was no bitter, knife-keen, deadly, fresh air to contend with there. The friendly Esthonians pulled off wet boots and socks, rubbed red and swollen feet, brought cup after cup of hot milk and tea.

When the Finns could swallow no more they rolled off the benches to join Vladimir on the floor where mats had been spread for them. There they lay all night and most of the next day, sleeping when every aching joint would let them.

By two o'clock the following afternoon, they were able to drag themselves out to a sleigh which they had hired to drive the remaining ten kilometers to Reval.

Reval was journey's end. They found friends to stay with, and rested, until a ship could be had to take them to Vasa where they joined Mannerheim's army.

6

Vaino's Adventure

ON the morning after Sven left, Fru Lundborg woke Vaino early.

"Get up and help me, son. I have decided to accept Froken Hjalmar's invitation, close up the house and move in to Brunnsparken. It is so near town."

Poor bedridden Froken Hjalmar had her troubles since the Revolution, for her maid had run off to join the Red army, like a lot of other silly girls, and she had to depend for care on the kindness of her neighbors. She had often begged Fru Lundborg to come and live with her but so long as Sven and Anniki might need their own home that had been out of the question.

"Now that the children can't get back," said Fru Lundborg as they packed, "I think that we shall be better off there. You will be nearer school, if school is open, and I may be able to find some work for myself."

By three o'clock that afternoon everything was ready. Valuables which could easily be carried away were loaded into the sleigh. Marta was sent home for a visit to her sister, about whom she had been worrying for the past two months. Even the pony was provided for. It was arranged that he should board in a nice stable in town, where there would be plenty of horses for companionship. It would be a pleasant, new experience for him.

They gave an old fisherman the back door key, and asked him to pay the house a daily visit, but they did not tell him, or anyone else, where they were going, and they drove off without looking back for fear of weakening their resolution.

When they arrived at the villa in Brunnsparken, they had hardly said how do you do to Froken Hjalmar, before Fru Lundborg left Vaino to unpack, and drove off on a mysterious errand to a mysterious house.

Vaino made himself very busy. His mother was to sleep upstairs within call of their frail hostess, and he had a little room off the main living room below. It was very cosy, with only one door which entered it out of the big room, and a little window which was really quite high, as the ground outside sloped away. Vaino could not help feeling relieved as he noticed that. One could be brave as a lion, but in those days one would rather not sleep by windows that men could easily climb

[207]

in and out of. One side of the room was entirely taken up by an old carved wardrobe of amazing proportions. He had just finished storing his few belongings in those capacious depths, when his mother came, looking hurried and determined, and marched straight upstairs to speak to Froken Hjalmar.

The room was at the head of the stairs, and although he did not mean to listen, Vaino could not help overhearing some of their conversation as he sat by the fire in the living room.

"I hope I am as patriotic as anybody," Froken Hjalmar, who like many deaf people spoke very loudly, was saying in a querulous voice, "but at my time of life, and in my health I don't want to take any risks. You can't be sure that things are going to be so successful as you think."

For a time they seemed to be arguing in whispers. Then Froken Hjalmar broke out again.

"Very well, my dear Anna. I don't care what you do here so long as I know nothing about it. I cannot leave my bed, and I won't take any responsibility."

That night Vaino had been asleep for some time when he was wakened by voices in the main room, and slipped out of bed to see what was the matter. His mother and two men were standing with their backs to him, talking in low tones.

"It is almost ideal," she was saying, "for the entrance is screened from the road, and none of the neighbors are near enough to see you come in and out. My friend can't get down stairs, and can't hear you, and you can feel quite sure of my little son. He has proved himself already."

Bursting with pride and torn with curiosity, Vaino closed his door softly and crept back to bed. The temptation to stay unseen was strong, but he had to justify his mother's confidence in him. In a few minutes he was glad that he had done so, for the door opened, and Fru Lundborg came in bringing the two men. Vaino jumped up.

"This is my son," she said.

The men shook hands with him gravely, as if he had been grown up, and Vaino stood as tall as possible, and looked right at them. He had grown four inches, during the last year, and indeed he felt very much older. Last March it was he who had clung to his mother, now she leaned on him. The men seemed satisfied, and turning away began to examine the cupboard.

"We shall be back tomorrow," said one, at last. They saluted and went out, with Fru Lundborg following them to the door.

Vaino did not dare to ask questions, but he could hardly get through the day. That night, however, he was bitterly disappointed, for his mother sat upstairs all evening, reading to Froken Hjalmar from a boring book, and insisted that he stay with her for fear he might be in the way. It was almost more than Vaino could bear.

When he finally went back to his room, the men had disappeared, his things were neatly laid out in piles on the floor, and the cupboard was locked. At the end of a week, however, they asked him to come in, and see their finished work.

They had built a false back to the cupboard, lined with shelves, on which they asked Vaino to put all his clothes, and tools and even the accordion. Under the bottom shelf was a small key hole, and when they turned the key the false back swung out, and Vaino saw a complete wireless and telephone outfit. Now he understood.

For several days after that the men, who were called Eric and Ahto, did not come, then one evening they arrived in high good humour.

"We've had a rare day!" said Eric. "You should have seen us, about eleven o'clock this

morning, dressed in a couple of telephone
linesman uniforms which we 'borrowed'
from the Russkys! We climbed some poles
in the middle of the street, and while people
passed below, and three of the Red Guard
stalked up and down, we sweetly whistled the
Internationale, and tapped the main cable between here and Reval."

They had led their wires out into the fields,
and back, underground, to the villa in
Brunnsparken!

Several nights later everything was ready
for the test. Vaino and his mother were allowed to sit with them while they tried to
put their first call through. They were all
trembling with excitement, as Eric swung
open the cupboard and made his connections.
At last there was a voice.

"Reval? Is this Reval? This is Helsingfors."

To their horror they realized that Eric
was talking to the Red Headquarters, who

must also be trying to reach Reval on the same line! Eric had to think very quickly. He pretended not to have understood them, and said in German:

"When Hauptmann comes to Libau send him on according to plan. Is this Regulus in Libau? Who is that? This is Major Blix, Reval."

"This is not Libau," answered the Red, joyously, excited to think that he was at last in touch with the outside world, "this is Helsingfors."

"Geh zum Teufel!" shouted the apocryphal Major Blix, and slammed down the receiver.

It was amusing to feel that they had fooled the Reds, but it was a bitter disappointment to find them on the line, for it meant that most of the work had to be done over. Next day, Eric, after some consultation, decided to cross to the other side of the Bay, and start from there. The nocturnal trips were over for the moment.

Those were dark times. It was almost impossible to get authentic news from the outside world. Fru Lundborg read "The Workman," which was filled with false Red triumphs and unbelievable White atrocities. Little sheets from a secret source which reported Mannerheim victories were almost as disturbing, for they nearly always turned out to be untrue. Of course there was no word from Sven or Anniki, and no hope of any.

The only cheerful side was that the Reds were having their troubles, too. The Russian soldiers kept demanding more and more pay.

"It is absolutely forbidden to soldiers in the Red or Russian army to sell weapons or ammunition to the enemy," announced "The Workman," one morning. Also, "By Order. Generals must go to the front with their troops."

Then one morning Vaino had an adventure which gave him gooseflesh for weeks afterward. He was out walking, and had

just turned into Brunnsparken suburb, when
he met two of the Red Guard. He greeted
them in Finnish as usual, and started to walk
unconcernedly past them, when one of them
grabbed him by the arm.

"See here. Aren't you that Vaino Lundborg who lives with his mother out on the
Borgo road?"

"Yes," said Vaino, with what Vladimir
would have called his "little enemy" face.
One of the guards was a stocky worker, so
broad that he was almost square. The other
was lean and tall, with hungry eyes. He spoke
like an educated man.

"I told you so," said the thick one. "Faces
is what I don't forget. I saw this kid and his
mother one day last March when we chased
a Russian officer out to their house. I've
always thought there was something phoney
about how that man got away."

"I have heard of the family," answered
the other. "They have already been reported

[215]

as contra-revolutionists. There is an older boy
and a girl."

The thick one turned back to Vaino.

"Haven't you a brother?"

"Yes."

"Where is he?"

"I don't know. He hasn't been home for a
long time."

"Gone with the Whites has he?"

"I can't say."

"You know more than you want to tell,
I'll bet," went on the thick one, shaking
Vaino to and fro. "Spill it, or you'll be sorry."

Vaino did not answer, and the Red gave
his arm a twist that made him bite his lip.
"Come now, young fellow. Tell what you
know, or you'll find yourself taking a walk
over the ice one of these mornings."

The Reds were using the ice in those days
as an execution ground. They marched out an
occasional suspect, and marched back without
him. The ice told no tales, and when it
melted, left no traces.

"I have nothing to tell you," answered Vaino, sullenly.

The lean guard interfered. "You'll never get much useful information that way, comrade. Let me talk to him. Young man, you and I might as well be friendly, see? Tell us where your sister is, and there will be several Finnmarks for you."

Vaino felt so enraged that he was afraid of bursting into tears, but he realized that a great deal depended on his behaviour.

"She went to Tammerfors," he said. "I don't know where she is now."

"That's more like it. Now where is the brother?"

"I can't say, I tell you. He hasn't been home in a long time."

"Have you ever overheard your mother talking to suspicious people?"

"What do you mean? My mother wouldn't have anything to do with suspicious people."

"Have you ever heard her express any contra-revolutionary sentiments?"

"What are they? She tells me legends about old Finland, if that is what you mean."

The thick one was getting impatient. "Bring him along to headquarters. They'll make him squeal if he has anything to squeal about."

"Let him alone," said the other. "He's too young for that, and you will only get yourself into trouble. I'll make a bargain with you, young Vaino. If you get any news about that brother and sister of yours, or if you hear anything interesting, and you come and tell me, Number 104 at the Kasernetorv, there will be a nice piece of money for you. Here is something in advance."

Vaino looked at the dirty bills that he was pulling out of his pocket. "All right. Only I don't think I should take anything until I get you some real information."

"As you like," answered the Red. "Now run along. No double crossing. You are going to be watched, remember."

Vaino obeyed the instructions to run very literally. All of his training to be a runner was used to put distance between him and the Reds. He ran back into the town, doubled on his tracks once or twice, and when he was sure that he had thrown off any possible pursuit darted into a schoolfriend's house, and telephoned his mother.

"You mustn't come back here," she said. "Go to the hotel, and I will meet you there as soon as I can."

Inside of three hours she drove up with all their things again packed into the sleigh. By night they were installed in cheap lodgings under new names. If they were suspected they could not ask any of their friends to run the risk of taking them in. Fru Lundborg said that she had arranged for Eric's sister to stay with Froken Hjalmar. They must not go near the villa in Brunnsparken again. Even the pony changed his boarding house.

Vaino did shed tears of rage that night,

when he told his mother how the Reds had tried to buy him. Fru Lundborg shook her head.

"Poor children," she said, "they have been without money for so long that when they get it they think it all powerful. I am glad you were not won by the golden bride."

"That sounds like a story," said Vaino, cheering up a little.

"It is, but I am too sleepy to tell it now. You shall have it in the morning if you will remind me of it."

In the morning they decided not to go out of the house for a couple of days in case the Reds might be looking for them when they found that the house on the Borgo road was deserted. Consequently, Vaino had his story.

―――――

The Golden Bride

I shall not try to tell you now how Ilmarinen and his bride lived joyfully together, like the cuckoos singing in the meadows, nor how he lost her, through the malice of beetle-browed Kullervo, the boy who was brought up crookedly, whom, on a day of frowning stars, he took into his service.

The Rainbow perished, and the days of Ilmarinen were darkened by a grief too deep and terrible for words. He could no longer see the sunshine, for sun and rain were now alike to Ilmarinen. Day after day, he sat on the threshold of his house, with his face in his hands, listening for a light footfall which never came. The dust of a month lay thick on his deserted anvil, and the spiders spun their webs over his copper hammer and the door of his forge. In the evenings he sat alone by the blackened ashes of an empty hearth and when at last he would climb into the built-in bed, it was not to sleep, but to lie tossing and pulling the red and white coverlet this way and that.

"I reach out for her in the night," said

Ilmarinen, "and she is not there. Nothing is there."

One day as he walked down the road, with the heavy and listless tread of an old man, not caring where he went, his feet led him past the deserted door of his smithy. There was no red glow in the heart of the forge, no sparks flying from the door, no cheerful noise ringing out, nor smoke curling up through the roof hole. Ilmarinen brushed aside the cobwebs and wandered in.

For some time he walked about inside, blowing off the dust here and there. Then he picked up his copper hammer, and balanced it lightly in his hand. Time passed, and Ilmarinen stood staring at his hammer and biting at his fist. At last he said, "I used to be able to make almost anything, in the old days. Why should I not make me a bride?"

With this thought some of his former energy returned and he began to hurry about, setting his place in order. He dredged the

streams for gold, and the marshes for silver,
and he cut down no less than thirty sledge
loads of wood, and made it into charcoal for
his furnace. He got his workmen together
again, and built up the fire.

When everything was ready he threw the
silver and gold into the oven and set his
workmen to blowing the bellows with all
their might. The sweat rolled down their
naked shoulders, but they did not work hard
enough to suit Ilmarinen, so he stripped to
the waist and set at it himself. In time the
metal began to take shape. Gradually it
formed, and the head of a ewe rose in the
flames.

"You might suit a wolf, but you are no
bride for me," said Ilmarinen, and shoved it
back into the fire, adding more metal to the
molten mass.

A second time the workmen blew with all
their might, a second time Ilmarinen was
not satisfied with their efforts, and a second
time he took the bellows out of their hands.

Then the shining head of a golden filly rose from the flames.

"A wolf might like you, but I don't," said Ilmarinen, and with a crushing blow of his hammer he dashed it down into the furnace.

For the third time the laborers set to work, for a third time Ilmarinen stirred the metal, and finally took the bellows out of their hands, and blew them himself. At last, and slowly, the head of a golden maid rose in the flames.

The more Ilmarinen worked the better he felt, and now as he saw the gleam of the golden bride, he flung back his head, and laughed as he used to do. The flames struck a golden radiance from her which played over his wet shining shoulders, his square white teeth and the smoke-blackened curls which fell across his forehead. The workmen fell back frightened by her streaming light but Ilmarinen seized her in his tongs, and tossing her out onto the anvil, began to work with might and main.

He fashioned feet for the golden bride, slim and delicate as flowers. They were beautiful to see, but they would not walk. He fashioned hands, long and pointed as the petals of water-lilies, but the hands would not embrace him. He set ears like shells on either side of her little head, and made a half-open mouth with tender curves, but no words of love came out of the mouth. He made eyes which shone like the moon and the stars, but said nothing with their shining.

Ilmarinen had sent his workmen away, and throughout the night he worked in the red light of his fire over the golden bride, thinking of new beauties which he could add to her. When the tops of the pine trees were black against the dawn the maiden was finished.

Ilmarinen laid down his hammer, carried her to the door of the smithy, stood her up and looked at her. The red streaks of the coming sun were no more beautiful than her shining. Her mouth was half-open as if to speak to him, but she said nothing, her hands were half out, but she stretched them no farther. Ilmarinen admired her for a long time, but she did not move. At last he ran his hand through his curls, and sighed.

"You would be beautiful if you had some sense, and could answer me," he said.

Then he picked her up on his shoulder, and set off to his house. When he reached home he wrapped her in his softest blanket, and laid her on the bed while he ran out to get the bath house ready. He felt cheerful again as he gathered wood and made the fire, heated the stones and fetched the water. The first snow flakes of the winter fell about him when he came out. He went to the house, got the golden girl, and carried her back to the bath. There he washed her tenderly until she was free from ashes and the sooty marks of the forge.

"You might be nice to me, you see I do everything for you," said Ilmarinen, but the golden bride did not answer.

Ilmarinen then washed himself until his skin was as white as it had been on the day of his marriage with the Rainbow, and his hair shone like that of the golden girl herself. When he was clean he ran out and rolled in the new fallen snow, then went back and switched himself briskly with the bath whisks.

He felt so well that he could not help being cheerful as he went into the house, with the golden bride on his shoulder. He spread the best blanket on the bed, and the best coverlet over it, and laid the golden bride between them. It was dark by the time he had finished, so he climbed into the bed himself and lay down by the side of his maiden of gold.

She was cold, ice cold from the head of her to the feet of her. There was not a warm spot on her anywhere. Ilmarinen shivered, and tucked the coverlets in between them. All that night the wind howled around the house, and the first flakes of snow drifted in under the door. Ilmarinen got up time after time, and gathered all the blankets he could find, and all the wolf and bear skins he possessed, to pile on top. In spite of his pains, however, when he woke in the morning his left hand, which had lain over the heart of the golden girl, was black with frost.

Ilmarinen looked at her reproachfully while he rubbed his frost bitten hand with the snow, but she smiled up at him from the best blanket as brightly as she had done the night before. He laid his right hand on her but drew it back quickly, for the chill of her burnt like fire.

"I think you would be about right for Vaino, he is somewhat old and chilly himself," said Ilmarinen at last.

With that he drew on his woolen gloves, took her up on his shoulder and went off with her to Vaino. He set her down before him with some pride, for she was very fair to look upon, and he thought that Vaino would be pleased to have such a beautiful bride at last.

"What do you expect me to do with this golden ghost?" asked Vaino.

"I thought you would like her," said Ilmarinen. "She will look dovelike enough when you hold her on your knee, and I thought you were wanting a sweet little wife."

"My dear brother," said Vaino, "do take her and break her up in your furnace, or send her to the silly Russians, or to the Saxons, who prefer their spoils of battle to anything else, and fight over women as if they were coins. She doesn't suit me at all, for I have never been tainted with love of gold, nor longing after silver."

Then Vaino made a song, to warn young men never to fall in love with cold yellow metal, and some of it, as nearly as I can remember, ran like this:

"Young men beware of the golden snare,
Leave the cold of gold to bite the old,
For the breath of a maid is warm and
    sweet,

[229]

And the heart gives back an answering
    heat,
But the breath of silver is only frost,
A touch of that breath and youth is lost."

7

Victory

THE weary March gave way to April. Snow still lay in the streets of Helsingfors, ice still covered the bay, but the cold was no longer like the blow of a heavy fist, and here and there a green blade pierced the white covering, a promise that again there should be color in the world.

Vaino and his mother remained in their

lodgings. They looked up and down the street before they went in or out, they were careful never to be seen together, but they did not let their fears keep them at home.

Vaino had work of his own now. Every evening he went to a house in the center of town, under the very noses of the Reds, collected some typewritten sheets of paper, and ran about the dark cold city, in every direction except that of Brunnsparken, shoving them under doorways.

He was distributing copies of "Free Speech," the new White newspaper. The telephone connection with Mannerheim had been established through Reval, and true information could be had about the White army, and about the world beyond ice-enclosed Finland. The White leaders wished to share the truth with the people of Helsingfors. All the presses were in the hands of the Reds, but the self-appointed editor assembled his issue, had a friend make ten copies on the typewriter, and sent each of these to be copied ten times in their turn. The Reds raged, searched the city for multigraphing machines and confiscated every one of them, and the unsuspected typewriters ticked merrily on until the end of the war. Vaino was one of their messenger boys.

On the evening of April third, there was such news in the paper that Vaino, as he ran through the slush, felt wings on his feet instead of wool-lined rubber boots. He could hardly wait to get rid of his share of the copies and dash home to his mother. Of course that would be the night when his street was full of passers-by. He lurked around the corner, and ran twice past the house before he had a clear field, and could dart in. He stormed up the steep stairs and burst open the door. His mother had drawn the dark green, tasseled portières which divided their two rooms, and, ready for bed, was getting warm in front of the green tiled stove before she went into her cold bedroom. Vaino slept on the sofa.

"Mother!" he screamed with what was left of his breath after the stairs, and shook his copy of "Free Speech" at her.

She jumped to her feet, "There· was a rumour this afternoon. Is it true?"

There it stood in the paper, typed out in black and white. The Germans, the long awaited Germans, had really landed. They were really going to help! Their ships had filled the harbor of Hango that morning, the Russian garrison had hastily surrendered, the Germans had disembarked, and were still disembarking when the paper went to press.

"Think of it," cried Fru Lundborg, snatching the paper out of Vaino's hand. "Nine thousand of them, trained soldiers, war seasoned, with plenty of supplies and ammunition!"

That was almost as many as the whole White army, which had been collected with such haste, and such labor. How could the Germans spare them?"

"They've been planning for weeks," said Vaino, trying to read over his mother's shoulder. "They cut a channel in the ice two kilo wide, and swept all the mines out of it."

"Can't you see them? That fat little ice-breaker Sampo ahead, then the destroyers, and then three whole divisions of transports, with a cruiser escorting each!"

"No wonder the old Russians gave up the fortress when they saw all those ships!"

"Can't you hear the people cheering as they landed!"

Vaino and his mother threw their arms around each other, and began to jig for joy. Suddenly she stopped. "Heavens! I forgot the Reds on the first floor. They might hear us and come up to know what it is all about."

They bounced down, hand in hand, on the sofa. Fru Lundborg was flushed with excitement and exercise. With her long hair un-braided and flying about her head, she looked no older than Anniki.

"Isn't it good of the Germans? Isn't it

good of them to come and help us?" exclaimed Vaino.

Fru Lundborg, grown up again, began to collect her hair and twist it into sober plaits.

"They don't just do it for our blue eyes," she said. "Don't be sentimental, son, when there is a war on."

"Why then?"

"It is their best way to threaten Petrograd in case their peace with Russia does not last, or the Allies should arrive there. It is a flanking movement. . . ."

The week which followed the landing of the Germans was exciting, joyful, and terrible.

There was not a White in Helsingfors who did not throw himself into feverish underground activity. Weapons were smuggled to and fro, and collected in a central spot, secret meetings were held in candlelit cellars, everyone was whispering, sending messages, making plans.

The Germans advanced slowly along the

southern coast, meeting little resistance. Day by day they drew nearer, their progress interrupted only by occasional skirmishes. On April fourth the Whites in the East took Rautu, on the sixth, Mannerheim himself drove his offensive through Tammerfors, and captured the city. The White broom was sweeping the Reds back to the sea.

The Reds also redoubled their activity. "The Workman" published wild stories of victory, wilder menaces to contra-revolutionists. In Helsingfors there were more arrests than ever. Anyone might be suspected, seized, clapped into prison, or hurried out over the ice. From the outlying districts came rumours about wholesale massacres of prisoners. The Whites in Helsingfors rejoiced and dreaded in secret.

On the afternoon of the eleventh, Vaino was sitting by the stove pretending to study his neglected English, and his mother was pretending to knit a sock, but both of them kept jumping up to look out of the window, and listening for strange sounds. The Germans were just outside the town. No one knew what was to happen.

At four o'clock there was a very distant popping and sputtering.

"Surrender has been refused," said Fru Lundborg, and she handed Vaino his coat and cap from the hook behind the door.

They ran out into the empty street, but when they reached the market square by the harbour, they found a milling crowd of people, whispering, shifting. Members of the Red Guard were running toward the Kasernetorv, and cursing those who dared to question them. Fru Lundborg and Vaino shouldered their way through until they came to the house of a friend in a side street, where it had been arranged that some of the Whites should meet when the day came. Two families were there ahead of them. The men were going out to fight as soon as the Germans entered the city, and they wished to leave their wives and small children where they would have company, and a measure of protection.

It was one of the largest houses in Helsingfors. There was no fire in the drawing room because of a shortage of fuel, so they all squeezed themselves into the smoking room. No one went to bed that night. The small children were put to sleep on the sofas, the others sat up, talking, discussing. At about two o'clock, Vaino, curled up on a window seat, dozed off by accident.

He dreamed of thunder, and woke to find that the thunder continued. Only the children were left in the room, and they were frightened. The youngest, a little girl of two, began to cry and started one of the others. Fru Lundborg ran in and gathered three of them in her long arms to comfort them. Over their heads she spoke to Vaino.

"They are in Fredriksberg. Don't cry, babies. Your mothers will be here in a minute. Daddy is going out to work, and mummy is telling him good-bye."

The lamps were still lit in the room, but the sky outside was streaked with gray. It was five o'clock. Vaino ran into the cold drawing room and looked out on the street. It was gray and empty in the morning light. At the corner he could see the four men who had gone from that house, rifles hidden under their cloaks, swinging solemnly away. There was not much danger of meeting the Reds just then. They were all busy at Fredriksberg. Fru Lundborg had surrendered the comforted child to her mother, and followed Vaino into the drawing-room.

"If I could only fight!" she cried, striking the windowsill with her fist.

"Couldn't I go, Mother? Wouldn't they take me? I'm quite big now, you know."

His mother answered him with unwonted severity. "Certainly not. This is one day when there are plenty of us, and you are not needed at all."

Vaino sighed, and his breath came out like a cloud in the frosty room.

"It is too cold in here," continued Fru Lundborg, "I'm going down to the kitchen to make litres of soup. Someone is sure to need it. You could be very useful looking after the children, if you would. Come down in a little while, and I will give you some breakfast. Now mind there is no nonsense about running out in the street. Stay in the house."

Reluctantly Vaino followed her back to the smoking room.

The morning seemed timeless, interminable. Every second had a separate entity. Those who waited were conscious of their heart beats, of their breathing. An unexpected sound turned them cold, made them look at each other fearfully. It had been rumoured that the Reds meant to loot and burn the city if they were forced to abandon it. Even the little children felt the tension. They played quietly, stopping to climb into their mothers' laps, and find in bodily warmth reassurance for vague fears which they did not understand. An obbligato of firing ran through the day. Sometimes nearer, sometimes farther, never silent for long.

Those who could eat had finished their lunch when a burst of firing came from very near at hand. The women sprang up and started to lead the children down to the cellar. Vaino ran into the drawing room to look out of the window. What he saw sent him flying back to catch at his mother's arm, and gasping "Reds!" drag her with him down the steps.

A party of Reds were thundering at the great door through which one drove in from the street! Fortunately it was locked, but as Vaino and his mother ran out of the house into the carriage way the lock was beginning to give. They swung down the great iron bar which went straight across the door and made it fast at night, while the Reds beat with their rifle butts on the outside. Then they locked the door of the empty porter's room in case the Reds should break through the grated window, and ran back into the house. Fru Helen, the owner, met them and helped them fasten the bolts.

"If they get into the courtyard we are lost!" she said. "There are a dozen windows which they could break and climb through!"

"The carriage doors are very heavy. They will stand for a while. We must lock the lower rooms which give on the courtyard," answered Fru Lundborg.

It did not take long. The house was empty of servants. They had run away the day before.

"I suppose the children are safest locked in the cellar?" asked Fru Helen.

"If they don't burn the house down over us!"

When the two women had locked all they could they ran down the cellar steps. Vaino managed to hang behind, and slip back unobserved, to the drawing room. The prospect was not encouraging. The Reds had apparently fired into the lock and broken it but the bar still held. They were getting ready to make a concerted charge against one of the panels. It was only a question of time before it would give way.

Suddenly Vaino saw a new band of men run around the corner. There was a fusillade of shot. A bullet crashed through the window where he was standing and the glass flew around him. Vaino lost no time in dropping to the floor.

He lay there listening to the firing, the shouts, the running feet. There was one inhuman scream, and then an explosion which broke in another window pane and sounded like the end of the world. After that comparative silence, and a few distant shots, Vaino raised himself slowly to his hands and knees, somewhat surprised to find himself uninjured, and peered cautiously through the broken window. The lamp post outside was strangely twisted. The street was empty except for a Red who lay some distance away like a bundle of old clothes, thrown down in a hurry, and another in German uniform who was crawling slowly toward the house. Just then Fru Lundborg appeared in the doorway behind Vaino and asked, with fire in her eyes, why he had not come to the cellar with the rest. He beckoned her to the window. "Poor man!" she cried. "We must go and help him."

They ran together down the stairs. The iron bar had been bent and they had some trouble in getting the doors open. At last they got into the street, lifted the groaning German between them and carried him into the house. They had him on a sofa in the entrance hall, left him in the care of Fru Helen who then had come up from the cellar, and ran back to the Red. He was lying in a broad red pool which made Vaino feel rather sick. Fru Lundborg stooped over him, and turned him gently. The edge of her skirt trailed in his blood. "Too late," she said. "The bullet cut his throat." Then she let him fall back as he was and went with Vaino into the house. The German on the sofa had been moved into the dining room where it was warmer. The women were cutting his uniform away from the wound in his breast. He was groaning and coughing horribly.

"I must find a doctor," said Fru Lundborg jamming on her hat. "Vaino, go upstairs and take care of those children. No one else has time."

Vaino hated being relegated to the nursery instead of running for the doctor, but he was too wise to argue with his mother when time was precious. She did not give way easily. He climbed slowly to the smoking room, and by the time he had sullenly started the two oldest to cutting pictures out of a magazine, and angrily sung all the songs he knew to the younger ones, he heard his mother's voice and a man's below. He escaped from the children and ran downstairs. The doctor was bending over the very quiet German. He shook his head. Then with Vaino's help he carried the man into one of the maid's rooms, laid him on the bed, shut the door and left him there. At dusk a cart came along and collected the Red who had been lying in the street.

By night the men who had gone out that morning began coming back. One by one they drifted in until at last they were all there, all had been embraced, wept over, given some of Fru Lundborg's soup which had been simmering all day.

"It's finished," they said. "We have the city firm and fast."

It seemed too good. They were free! No more creeping in and out of houses, no more looking up and down the street before leaving a doorway, no more whispering, calling people by strange names, pretending not to recognize friends when one met them in the street; no more springing up at a sound in the night, trembling at footsteps behind, starting when a hand was laid on the shoulder.

The weeks that followed were filled with joy. One piece of good news after another came to the free city. The heart could scarcely contain them all. The Red government fled to Kotka. Mannerheim was driving down from the Northwest. On May fourth Kotka fell. The leaders of the Revolution escaped over the Bay to Russia, deserting their followers. The war was ended. Finland was free!

On the glorious May sixteenth Mannerheim entered Helsingfors at the head of his victorious army! The sun shone, the snow was gone, there were signs of buds on the bare branches of the trees! The people stood in the street and waved flags and handkerchiefs, threw flowers and shouted. The General, in his white fur hat, rode a prancing horse, and smiled and saluted on every side. Behind him marched his cavalry and his infantry, trained soldiers now, war seasoned, weary, but triumphant!

The parade swung through the principal streets, and came to a halt at the Square in front of the Senate House. There Mannerheim was received by the President of Finland and all the other dignitaries. There were speeches.

Fru Lundborg stood on a balcony with some of the women's committee, and Vaino was with her. When it was over she turned to him, her eyes shining with pride.

"I think Sven has gained a little weight," she said. "Didn't he march well?"

After the parade they all met, as had been arranged in the villa at Brunnsparken. Sven came first, banging Vaino on the back in the old way, and pretending to box with him. And then Anniki arrived, arm in arm with a lean and hardy Scarelius, weatherbeaten skin on his musician's hands, and rough hair cut. For the second time in his life, Vaino saw his mother weep, but these were tears of joy.

There was only one cloud in the sky. Vladimir had not come back. "It was at Tammerfors," said Sven. "He said he was not much hurt, and made us take him back to camp. Then he saw it was all over. He said he wasn't sorry, as he was so alone, but I wanted to bring him back, Mother. He could have had a home with us always, couldn't he?"

"Of course he could," said Fru Lundborg.

That night they had dinner in their own house on the Borgo road which Fru Lundborg had opened during the previous week. Afterwards they sat around the stove, for it was still chilly, although the snow had melted. Marta peered in the doorway from time to time, beaming at them. Anniki and her husband sat hand in hand on the sofa. Sven had stretched himself out in the easiest chair, enjoying to the full the luxury of doing nothing, and knowing that there was nothing to do. Vaino sat on the floor, ready to jump up and bring anyone anything and Fru Lundborg was sewing under the lamp, mending some of Sven's clothes, which he had brought home in the most dreadful condition.

"Tell us a story, mother," said Anniki. "Then we will know that the nightmare is ended, that we can forget it, that there can again be poetry and music in the world."

Fru Lundborg laughed. "The Finns are a great people," she said. "They have many troubles, but they wait, and they always win in the end. Shall I tell you how it came out in the olden days?"

* * *

The Capture of the Sampo

All through the long cold winter old Vaino, huddled by the glow of Ilmarinen's forge, brooded on a way of bringing food and warmth to his people. Day after day the fierce wind piled the drifts higher and higher about the smithy, and Ilmarinen dug a tunnel through the drift so that they could go in and out.

At last Vaino, clutching his long blue cloak about him with fingers that were stiff with frost, announced his decision. "We must go to Pohja, for the Sampo."

[251]

Ilmarinen straightened up from his work, and looked around.

"It is locked in the copper mountain," he said.

This was no news to such a magician as Vaino. He merely smiled, and answered, "I think we should go by boat."

"It is safer by land," said Ilmarinen.

"Think of the peace of a boat," chanted Vaino, "the smooth silent water, the soft singing wind, the high rocking ship."

Ilmarinen's face clouded. Vaino saw that he must be diverted.

"Let the boat go," he cried, "but do make me a sword!"

That was different. Ilmarinen had had nothing important to make for a long time. He beamed with pleasure as he gathered together silver and gold and copper, and melted and moulded and tempered the blade. When he had finished, the sword shone with the beauty of the sun and the moon and the stars, and in Vaino's hands, carved an iron moun-

tain as if it had been brown cheese. Then Ilmarinen made himself some armour.

They saw the long nights of winter slip
into the swift dusk of spring, and the spring
winds blew through their hair before at last
they harnessed their horses and set out for
Pohja. They had not gone far, when they
heard a weeping sound coming from the sea-
shore on their left.

"It is a maid or a dove," said Vaino, and
they turned their horses to go and see.

Where the white lip of the sea curved
back from the land, they found not a maiden,
nor a dove, but a fine high boat, lying on its
side, and creaking and groaning as if it had
all the sorrow in the world.

"Why do you grieve, wooden ship?" asked
Vaino.

"Reason enough," lamented the ship, "for
a boat longs for water as a maid longs for a
husband. When I was made they said I might
be a warship. They said I might go out to
battle every summer, and come back full of

booty. Now other boats, even bad ones, go three times a year, and I, though well made and graceful, have never gone at all. I lie here with the worst worms in the world crawling under my boards, and the worst birds building in my masts, and the worst toads hopping all over me. It isn't a life for a boat. I think I would have been two or three times better off if I had been left a fir on the mountain, with a squirrel in my branches, and maybe a puppy playing in my shade."

"What nonsense!" cried the boat, sharply, Clever old Vaino patted it soothingly, and looked it over with his shrewd old eyes.

"Take heart," he said. "Perhaps your builder gave you the power to move through the water without being rowed."

"What nonsense!" cried the boat, sharply, forgetting to weep. "Why we can't even get into the water without being pushed."

"I'll push you," said Vaino. "Will you go without oars then?"

"I never heard of such a thing," answered the boat, aggrieved.

"I suppose you could go if someone rowed you?"

At that the boat brightened. "Of course," it said, "and with the wind in my sails, too."

Vaino told the horses to graze and wait for him. Then he and Ilmarinen pushed the boat out to sea. Ilmarinen was so interested that he felt reconciled to the idea of a journey by water. The boat bounced joyfully up and down on the waves, making them slap against its sides, and blowing foamy bubbles.

"I could hold one hundred men!" it chuckled.

Vaino threw back his head and began to sing, with his white beard blowing in the spring wind like the white clouds above him, and the boat filled with the people of his song. There were young men with hard hands, maidens with tin on their heads, and old folk, who sat on the benches.

Vaino set them to rowing, but the boat did

not move. The dreams of Vaino were fair and
strong, but they could not drive the boat. At
last Ilmarinen strode through the dreams and
took the oars in his powerful fists. He gave a
strong pull, and the boat shot forward. Vaino
seized the rudder. With the oars hissing like
geese in the water and the stern croaking like
a raven, the boat flew past the headland on
which was the dwelling of Ahti.

Ahti had had a year of bad harvests, and
he nursed a grudge against Pohja because he
had not been invited to the wedding of the
Rainbow. When he saw Vaino and Ilmarinen
in the boat he persuaded them to take him
along, and climbed in with an armful of
planks.

"What are they for?" asked Vaino.

Ahti winked. "Foresight won't sink a ship,
nor a prop overturn a haystack," he said.

So they were three heroes who journeyed
to Pohja.

For a time all went well. When they came
to a cataract they passed it safely by means of

a charm which Ahti had learned in the river of Tuonela, and which Vaino wove into a song.

> "Cataract's daughter,
>   Gather the water.
> Heap up the foam,
>   Gather it home.
> Hold it firm and hold it fast,
> Until our boat is safely past."

A little later their keel stuck on a giant pike. Ahti was sure that he could kill it, but failed through overconfidence, fell into the water himself and had to be pulled out by the hair.

"Some people think they are grown up when they aren't," grumbled Ilmarinen, and struck at the pike. His sword broke in his hand.

"Takes a man for this work," said Vaino, smiling sweetly at the other two. He speared the pike, brought it in, and cut in half. They ate it for breakfast, lunch and dinner, and when they had finished Vaino made a harp for himself from the jaws, a kantele, filled with magic. Ilmarinen could not play it, Ahti drew from it only jangling sounds. Vaino quietly put it away until he should have need of it.

In due course they reached the misty shores of Pohja, drew their ship up on the rollers, and strode up to Louhi's hall. Louhi was not pleased to see the three of them together, but when she began to question them, Vaino showed her his pike kantele, and that stopped her for a time, since it was like nothing else on earth.

All of the young people, all of the old people, all of the men, all of the women, and all of the children in Pohja tried their skill at playing on the new kantele. They strummed and hummed, they twanged and plucked, but not a tune could any of them get from it. After several days an old blind man, who had been trying to sleep near the fire, got up, grumbling and mumbling, and shoved his way into the midst of them.

My hair is on end with your squawking,"
he said. "There's been no rest here for a
week. Since not a one of you can play the
thing, why don't you cast it back into the
sea?"

The kantele, which until now had been
silent, spoke for the first and last time.

"I will play for my creator," it said.

With one accord they handed it to Vaino.
Vaino smiled, and called for fresh spring
water to wash his hands. Then he seated himself on the singing stone, the stone of joy, and
spread his blue cloak around him in graceful
folds. He took up the harp and began to
sing.

At the first muffled notes, all the four-
footed things of the woods, with paws as soft
as the music, crept in to hear the singing. The
quick deer ran with the squirrels on their
backs, the wolves streaked like shadows from
their distant lairs, the honey footed bears
lumbered through the heather. They gathered peacefully in the courtyard, so many

that the weight of their furry bodies pushed over the fences. From a distant hill the forest people listened to the song, and the mistress of the forest, in her blue stockings with the crimson garters, climbed a tree to catch the soft sounds which floated up to her.

As the quick notes fluttered up and down the strings all the little singing birds of the air came and whirred about Vaino, lighting on his shoulders. The hawks soared high and harmless in the sky above, and the eagle left her young in the nest to listen. The daughters of the air, weaving gold and silver light into a fabric, paused as they floated by on clouds with rosy borders, and the shuttles fell from their dreaming hands, and were broken.

Then the music changed to the low roll of the sea, the sighing of the water along the shore. All the white and silver fishes, the salmon, the pike, the powan, swam to the land's edge to listen. Ahto, king of the sea, with his long green beard of sea-weed, climbed up on a lily pad, and his daughters, sisters of the slender reeds which blow along the margin, ceased to comb the snaring tresses of their long soft hair.

Vaino sang of sorrow. In the halls of Pohja not one eye was dry, not one of those who listened refused to weep. He sang of sorrows that might come to Suomi, and his own tears rolled down his cheeks, for even he was forced to weep at the song. The tears rolled down his beard, over the floor, out the doors, and into the lake. Then the duck dived deep, and came up with a mouthful of pearls, and the pearls were the tears of Vaino.

Vaino had finished singing. Louhi, who had listened and wept, could not be put off any longer. She asked the heroes why they had come to Pohja.

"To tell the truth," said Vaino, "we want to share the Sampo with you."

"Three men cannot share a squirrel," croaked Louhi.

"Have it your own way," answered Vaino,

"but if you will not give us half, we will take the whole."

Without waiting to hear more, Louhi rushed to the door of the house, shaking her withered fists in the air, and screaming at the top of her lungs for all the swordsmen in the village. Before they could snatch up their weapons, Vaino began to sing. He sang a merry song, and the men who had come to kill him were seized with such laughter that they could not stand up, but fell on their knees in the doorway. Then he sang a sleepy song, and all the heroes of Pohja, the old men, the maidens, even the little children, fell into a deep and dreamless slumber. Vaino took sleep needles from his pocket, and sewed their eyelids tightly together. Then he and the other two went off to get the Sampo.

It was not an easy matter, for the copper mountain was locked with nine locks. Vaino sang, Ilmarinen worked, and so at last they entered. The Sampo was rooted with three roots, one in the earth, one in the sea, one in the hill. Even Ahti could not tear it up. At last they got a bull and plowed around it. When it had been loosened they dragged it out, and carried it to their boat.

For three days, swiftly and quietly, but well content, they sailed over the water at a gay pace. Then Ahti began to grumble.

"The last time I rowed there were songs to help the rowers. Now there is only a gloomy silence."

"Songs would make us slow," answered Vaino. "We must travel swiftly while the golden daylight lasts."

"Time is passing at its own pace," said Ahti. "Silence will not keep black night from falling."

Vaino made no answer, and for a day Ahti kept quiet, then the silence irked his lively soul, and he again urged Vaino to sing. Vaino was firmer than ever.

"Time enough for rejoicing, when we have brought the Sampo safely home."

But Ahti could not be restrained. "I'll sing myself!" he shouted, and rushing to the stern of the boat, he began. He stretched his mouth and roared, wagged his chin and tossed his head. The songs he made with all this effort were so noisy and discordant that people all along the shore put their fingers in their ears. A crane, sitting on a stump, counting the toes on its left foot, rose screaming with fright into the air. No crane before or since has ever been so frightened as that one was. He flew and he screamed until he came to Pohja, and his screaming wakened the Lapps from their sleep.

Louhi ran out of the house, rubbing her eyes. She could soon see what had happened. Her corn and her cattle were untouched, but her copper mountain was broken open, and the Sampo was gone. She grew so weak with rage that she raised her hands to heaven, and called on the Maid of the Mist, Iku, the sea-serpent's son, and Ukko himself, to help her.

To and fro through the air the Maid of

the Mist shook her pearly sieve, filled with
fine drops. A dense fog from the water, a
thick cloud from the sky, folded Vaino and
his ship in their clammy embrace so that he
could not stir for three days.

"This is no ordinary fog," he said at last,
and he ran his sword through the mist, and
stabbed at the surface of the sea. Mead
dripped from his sword, and the mist lifted
slowly, and floated away through the sky.

They had just made haste to set their sails
and move forward when they heard a roaring in the water beside them, and saw jets
of spray whirling over the boat. Ilmarinen,
strongest of men, looked out, and cowered
back, covering his eyes with his cap like a
frightened child. Vaino hurried to the edge
of the ship. In the water splashed Iku, the
sea-serpent's son, the evil thing of the sea!

If Vaino had felt fear, if he had hesitated,
they would have been lost, but he did not. He
seized Iku by the ears, and dragging him so
far out of the water that he was powerless,

shook him to and fro as a dog shakes a rat, shouting, "How dare you show your ugly self to man?"

Iku had never had such a greeting before. When Vaino paid no attention to his frightful teeth, but repeated the question three times, Iku grew afraid, and answered sullenly, "If you will let me go I will promise you never to do it again."

Then Vaino, with a final shake, flung him back into the sea, and that is why no other man, even to this day, has ever seen Iku, the sea-serpent's son.

The heroes still had Ukko to contend with, Ukko, who sends help to all who ask him. Ukko called to the winds, and they rose in fury. They stripped the needles from the pines, the tassels from the grass, the flowers from the heather, and they lashed the waves until they towered above the little boat.

Vaino cried out in sorrow, when his kantele was washed away, and Ilmarinen cursed the day when he had deserted dry land to set his foot on the heaving wood of the vessel. Ahti began to build up the side of the boat with his planks until they were higher than the waves, and Vaino begged the winds to help them. Thus they withstood the tempest.

By now Louhi had had time to gather her warriors, pack them into a great ship, and start in pursuit. Vaino felt the winds of ill omen blow through his hair, and he told Ahti, the active one, to climb to the top of the mast and see what he could see.

"There is a cloud on the horizon," said Ahti.

"That won't be a cloud. Look again."

"There is an island, where the sky meets the sea."

"That won't be an island. Look again."

Ahti looked, and what he saw nearly brought him tumbling down from the high mast. "It is Louhi with a boat full of warriors!" he cried.

Then Vaino and Ilmarinen tried with all their strength to speed the boat over the

water, but no matter how they tried, Louhi
in her large swift ship drew steadily nearer.
Vaino took a piece of tinder from his tinder
box, and threw it over his shoulder, saying a
charm.

"May this become a reef,
And bring the ship to grief."

No sooner said than done. A cliff rose up
in the water so suddenly that the ship could
not turn in its course. The ship struck and
shivered, the splinters flew in the air like
leaves brought down by a tempest. Louhi
leapt out and built herself wings from the
fragments. In the shape of an eagle with iron
talons, she soared aloft, carrying one hundred men on each of her great pinions.

Vaino had seen the wreck, and with a
lightened heart he had turned to his rowing,
taking no time to look behind him. Now the
spray which flew from the stern of his boat
shaped into the white form of the Water
Mother herself, who called to Vaino in a
voice as soft as the mist.

Vaino turned, and saw, not the Water Mother, dissolving into foam, but the black wings of Louhi, bristling with warriors, blotting out the sun.

Though he had little hope, he nodded to her, and said, "Well, Louhi, are you ready now to share the Sampo?" The others fell to praying for shirts of fire to turn the spears.

Louhi screamed like an eagle, and swooped down with outstretched claws. Ahti struck at her, but she swerved, and laughed at him. Vaino, unable to reach his sword, tore the rudder from its moorings, swung it through the air, and crashed into her claws as she perched on the mast. She reeled to one side, losing her hold. One hundred warriors dropped into the sea from her wings, as a squirrel drops from the boughs of a fir-tree. With her remaining claw she clutched the Sampo, and tried to rise with it into the air, but she could not hold it. It shattered on the side of the boat, and the fragments fell into the water.

The larger pieces sank to the bottom,
where the daughters of Ahto gathered them
lovingly. From them comes the unfailing
wealth of Ahto's kingdom. The waves bore
the rest to the shores of Suomi, save for one
tiny bit which fitted under Louhi's claw.

Vaino shouted for joy when he saw part of
the Sampo washed ashore on his own land,
and Louhi, still hovering above, heard him,
and screamed her answer.

"A curse on your plowing and frost on
    your sowing!
I'll blight all your cattle, and keep them
    from growing!
I'll steal away your moon and sun,
And lock them up till life is done.
    I'll call the bears,
    From their lairs
    To eat your mares.
You shall all of you perish from sickness
    and dearth,
Till the name of your race is forgotten
    on earth."

[270]

"I've never been afraid of Laplanders," answered Vaino.

Then Louhi went home with her morsel of the Sampo, and to this day the Northland is a land of meager harvest. Vaino sowed in the earth the fragments which the waves had cast on the shores of Suomi, that they might bring forth rye for bread, and barley for ale. As he sowed them he called upon Jumala, saying:

"Be thou a castle of stone to us against
    our enemies,
Be thou a fence of iron about us against
    our enemies,
Give us harvest and joy, and long life in
    our beautiful Suomi."

So did Vaino anew bring food and peace to his people, singing.

THE END.

Bibliography.

Kalevala; The Land of the Heroes. Translated by W. F. Kirby, E. P. Dutton, and other translations of the Kalevala.

La Revolution Rouge de Finlande, en 1918. Henning Soderhjelm, Librairie Payot, Geneva.

La Guerre D'Independance en Finlande en 1918. Ignatius & Soikkeli, Societé Otava, Helsingfors.

Dä Pojkarna Drogo ut. Kurt Reuter, Holger Schildt, Helsingfors.

Kamp och Aventyr i Röda, Finland, Thure Svedlin, Holger Schildt.

Dä Finland's Öde Avgjördes, Soderstrom & Co., Helsingfors.

And thanks are also due to Rurik Lindberg of Helsingfors.